DORM

S. K. HOLDER

ISBN: 9781917958004

www.rogghornpress.com

Part 1

Fortification

Chapter 1

The planet of Odisiris lies in the Andromeda Galaxy. It is home to a superhuman race known as Citizens...

Skelos Dorm's Stores were the envy of all the scientists in the City of Pareus. Constructed of cylindrical glass and steel, the fifty-storey, scientific research facility was devoted to the exploration and acquisition of Intelligent Systems. The windows were masked. You could see out, but you seldom saw in.

He had a fleet of staff to do his bidding. There were too many names to remember. Students, field researchers, professors, doctors, engineers, and scientific board members were in frequent attendance. He had one floor for specimens alone and a whole floor devoted to his work in neurorobotics.

He worked in the hub on the ground floor. The hub was his personal laboratory: his nervous system. And he was the brains. Each piece of research generated in the hub gravitated up. He had fashioned a section into his secondary living quarters. After all, he spent more time in the Stores than he did anywhere else. It was the place where he felt most at home, squeezed into his black lab coat and surgical gloves.

He swiped at the holograms that hovered above the raised podium.

His new, sixteen-year-old, apprentice watched him from a distance.

'May I have a look?' said the apprentice. He crept up to the platform, flicking his fringe out of his eyes.

Every year, he acquired one eager apprentice to work alongside him, to observe, to learn, to strive, and to emulate his great work, though none had ever achieved such a feat. Unfortunately, this apprentice was not of his choosing and was more tiresome than eager.

In fact, Skelos thought him rather stolid for a First Status Citizen. He seemed to care more about his looks and the females on his roster than he did about science, but the boy's father was a prominent figure in the Parliamentary Elite, so Skelos had no choice in the matter.

'No, you may not.' He tried to recall the boy's name. *Imbecile* sprung to mind. *No that's not it.* 'And please do me the courtesy of addressing me by my formal title.'

'Sorry Dr Skelos.' The young apprentice gulped. 'I'm eager to learn.'

'You're not as eager to learn as I was when I was your age. What do you do when you leave here?'

'Urm...er...'

Skelos rolled his eyes. He knew how he spent his time at sixteen years of age, and it wasn't chasing after girls.

Skelos's parents had encouraged him to enter the family energy business. Dorm Presteria Energy had been in his family for generations. He saw little point in working hard in a vocation he had no interest in and little understanding. The burden of this obligation had shifted to his older brother who was glad to take up the mantle.

He fell into his current profession when he was given the opportunity to work as an apprentice in the Pareusians's Pharmaceutical Stores. He found mixing toxic liquids together therapeutic and the clinical feel of the labs exhilarating. He remembered the rush he felt when he shrugged in and out of his tailor-made lab coat. He soon decided that he wanted to be a scientist, not just any scientist, the most renowned scientist in the world.

While he embodied science, his new apprentice treated it as if it were a punishment. *Well, I will see him punished.*

'Consult my notes.'

'That can't take very long. I seldom see you take any.' Skelos dragged a hologram of a brain in front of the Citizen youth. 'Dissect it.'

The apprentice prodded at the image as if it were a real brain. He then paused mid-prodding to gawp at a female research assistant who had wandered into their midst. Her hair cascaded down her back like a rapidly flowing river, and her eyelashes were decorated with ice crystals. The boy's eyes bulged with delight, and he twisted his neck, pursuing her in his mind.

Skelos considered slapping the boy around the head to garner his attention and then remembered who his father was. He made a fist of his slapping hand and watched the boy tweak apart the holographic brain segment by segment. The apprentice's name then came to him: *Imbrecas.*

'Well tell me what you're looking at, Imbrecas.' There was nothing to stop him having two apprentices, he supposed. *A second apprentice on alternate days of the week will alleviate this torture. I will speak to the boy's father tomorrow. See if we might come to another arrangement that is more to my advantage and less to his.*

'The-the left temporal lobe,' said Imbrecas, his hand shaking. 'Erm...the...Occ-occipital Lobe.'

Skelos sighed. His mind ventured to more critical matters. His years of measured research taunted him. By all accounts, they were non-productive. It was not his fault, or the fault of his assistants. It was *The Establishment.* They were to blame for his lack of progress. He could have Stores half the size of Pareus and a thousand discoveries and inventions to his name, but few would ever make it into Odisirian society, few would ever be recognised, rewarded or acknowledged, not without the backing of *The Establishment,* the three most powerful orders in Odisiris: The Parliamentary Elite, The P.D.P.C: Planetary Data Protection Committee, and the P.S.R.F.D: Pareus Scientific Research and Funding Division.

Skelos had an aptitude for neuroscience. The Establishment was impressed with his work in neurorobotics. Anything to do with droids and cyborgs was always welcome. However, they did not have the same enthusiasm when it came to understanding the Citizen psyche, reading thoughts, interpreting minds.

He understood their caution. Many Citizens had plenty to hide. They did not want their indiscretions made known to anyone but their closest allies.

Skelos grew weary of the protocol and rules regarding the research conducted within his Stores. His so-called Mind Work was done in the evening or at night when most of his team had gone home. There were ways in which he could take his Mind Work to another level. He was wasting his efforts experimenting on Unmarked Ones[1] and rodents. Their genetic make-up was different, very different to Citizens. Practically alien.

---

[1] Unmarked Ones – non-Citizens

He left Imbrecas to his dissecting. He crossed the grooved floor and accessed his private room. The specimen lay in a life-chamber, which allowed it to breathe. This particular specimen was a male Outsider of about eleven years. His bones were stiff and thin. His skin was bone white. His lips were blue, which Skelos found captivating as he was not a Citizen. The boy was brain dead: a repercussion of another one of his failed experiments. And there were many. The child would be the last Outsider he would use for his research, he concluded. He sighed and disconnected the life-chamber.

The door swung open. One of his assistant's wandered in: Denlor. He was the only one who had access to the private room.

'I've shut it off,' said Skelos, not looking behind him. He had worked with the Citizen for eight years and knew his noisy breathing and ponderous footsteps by heart.

'It was the right thing to do,' said Denlor. 'We need to find more compatible subjects.'

Skelos turned to face Denlor. Two years his senior, his eyes were the colour of wheat, and he had a deep cleft in his chin. Skelos had never socialised with the reputable Third Status Citizen outside of his Stores. He struggled with the idea of socialising with a Citizen whose blood was so orange that when he blushed, he resembled overripe fruit.

His mother detested the Lower Status Citizens. She considered them subservient and less intelligent than the First and Second Status Citizens. They often undertook menial roles. However, they could be counted on for their discretion. Skelos had vowed that when he grew up, he would embrace them as his equal and make some his friends. To date, he lacked the fortitude to make it happen. Like his mother, he preferred to spend his leisure time with the upper echelons of his society, the highborn First Status Citizens whose blood colour more closely matched his own.

'What is more compatible with a Citizen than another Citizen? I should make myself a test subject.'

'You're the only one who can interpret the results.' Denlor folded his arms behind his back and stared into the life-chamber. 'This is your work. If anything were to happen to you, there would be no one to carry on.'

How right Denlor was. 'You are one of the few who see merit in this work.'

'I see potential, yes, but I also see time and resources wasted on these Outsiders. Better to use amphibians than these creatures.' He nodded at the life-chamber. 'You find them fascinating?'

Skelos nodded and peered into the life-chamber with the eagerness of a child looking into a candy store. 'Look at the lips. Why blue when its blood is red?'

'This is what their genetic make-up dictates,' said Denlor, crossing his arms. 'Such creatures do not fascinate me. They are inhuman.'

'You don't think I should give up?' He didn't need Denlor's reassurance, just his undulant praise and appreciation.

'You give up when you're dead.'

'Could be a long time coming, if ever, if I have my way.'

Denlor smiled. 'What should I do with his body?'

This was what Skelos liked about Denlor. He was always willing to assist. Whatever the consequences. Whatever the subject matter.

'Toss it in the incinerator.' Skelos turned to leave. He paused at the door, remembering his Third Status Citizen vow. 'And Denlor—' *I will ask him over for an evening meal.*

'Yes?'

I can't do it. My beloved wife, Nylthia, will loathe me for it. Besides, what shall we talk about?

'Decontaminate the life-chamber when you're done.'

Skelos returned to his apprentice. Imbrecas had reassembled the brain and was now poking around one of his encrypted files.

Skelos decided he needed to keep a closer eye on him. The youth's father was Onas Pralyeton, one of the vice-chancellor's most championed advisers. Onas may have asked his son to spy on him. It stood to reason that any research Skelos conducted would be of a political advantage. *Let him poke around all he likes. He won't find anything. Not in here.*

As he approached the prying apprentice, a cyborg leapt from the third floor into the hub. The carbonic metal cyborg was a prototype for the new generation. Someone or something had attempted to deconstruct it. The layer of living tissue that covered it had been stripped away. Its teeth had been removed. Half its skull hung open, revealing part of a human brain, glistening like intestines within. A portion of its chest had been ripped open, exposing metal and tubes sloshing with fluid.

'Model ZT289 I believe,' said Skelos, gazing at the fusion of metal, wires, and tubes. The cyborg stood straight, its arms swinging. It stared at Skelos through infra-blue laser eyes. The last time Skelos had seen Model ZT289, they had had quite a pleasant conversation. It had given him a weather report and complimented him on his new lab coat. It appeared to have nothing to say to him today.

Imbrecas's scream pierced his ears.

'Never fear Imbrecas,' said Skelos. 'This one's friendly. Give us a moment, and we'll get him back in his tank.' He glanced in Imbrecas's direction and saw his feet poking out from underneath the hologram podium.

'What's going on up there?' Skelos turned his back on the cyborg. He gazed up at the third- floor balcony. He saw no merit in reasoning with a damaged machine. 'How many more of these models are you going to destroy?'

Several black coats looked over the balcony but did not appear in any hurry to proffer an explanation or a solution.

The cyborg fired a shot. It went over his head. He whirled to see the cyborg's arm raised. He jumped out of the way as it fired another four shots straight at him.

Skelos had insisted that the prototype's speed match that of a Citizen's, which meant it was exceedingly fast. He headed for the hologram podium. He gallantly leapt on top of it in the mistaken belief that the additional height would give him an advantage. The cyborg charged at him. It fired two more shots that blew holes in a paramount viewing screen, igniting it in a plume of flames. The fire alarm sounded with a deafening clang.

Skelos bounded from the podium as the cyborg's clunky metal foot smashed into the side of it. The hologram brain and confidential database shuddered and turned an opaque blur.

Imbrecas scurried from under the podium and sprinted through a set of glass doors and up the nearest stairwell. Skelos attempted to do the same.

'Automatic emergency lockdown initiated,' a male voice controller announced into the hub. 'Exits secured.'

Skelos slammed his hands against the exit doors and then groped his way to a steel pillar. Now this was getting humiliating. He knew how to override the lockdown system. He also knew how to disarm the cyborg. He had the ability to control technology with the power of his mind. But he had an audience. He heard them shouting from the balcony, which meant he would have to do things the laborious way. He seized a small gun, used for stabilising cyborgs, from a holster on the wall. He fired. It hit the cyborg in the chest, splitting apart a bundle of tubes and wires. Sparks and liquids spurted from the open cavity. The prototype staggered to a halt and cranked its weapon-arm.

And then it came at him again.

It punched the steel pillar. Skelos ducked and dashed to his private room. He dove through the door as soon as it opened. The lights came on and the door clicked shut after him. He activated the comms device on his wrist and made contact with one of the neurorobotics department supervisors. 'Who authorised this model to be armed?' he spat. 'Get the thing contained!'

A splash of blood landed on the device. Skelos wiped it off and rushed to a mirror. He had a nasty gash on his forehead, which was healing nicely, vanishing before his eyes. He used the heel of his hand to mop up the last trickle of blood descending towards his left eye before grappling his way to the back of the room, leaving blue blood stains and fingerprints along the length of the decontaminated life-chamber.

The cyborg made a bid to smash its way through the steel door. A dent appeared in it. Then another, deeper than the first.

Skelos felt feverish. His blood seemed to boil in his ears. He held his breath, his heart hammering. He closed his eyes and tried to level his concentration at the machine on the other side of the door. He pounded his forehead with his fist. Even away from prying eyes, he couldn't focus. And then he remembered the cyborg was fitted with the brain of a dead Citizen and that brain must still be functioning, or else—

The hammering ceased. Skelos heard a grating sound.

Finally. He snorted with relief and made his way over to the door. He opened it a fraction. An old sentinel cyborg overpowered the prototype. Twice its size, it was all machine and no brain. It leaned over Model ZT289 and smashed its elbow into its gaping chest. Fire erupted from it. The old cyborg then ground its foot into the prototype's skull with his steel boot. Fluids and grey matter leaked out across the laboratory floor.

Two men in lab coats appeared, brandishing fire extinguishers. As they proceeded to put out the fire, Skelos stepped from the room.

Imbrecas re-emerged through the shattered exit doors, gaping at Skelos. 'Friendly you said.'

'Minor mishap,' he replied. It wasn't the first time one of his prototypes had got out of control. He predicted it would not be the last.

Chapter 2

Skelos's wife was a gaunt-faced Citizen of forty-eight years. Eleven years Skelos's senior, Nylthia was an intelligent woman and one who had appreciated his intellect and ambition from the beginning. For she too was ambitious.

They were a perfect match, perhaps not in matrimony, but certainly in business. They hadn't shared a bed for six of the fifteen years they'd been together. They slept in separate wings of their estate. They saw each other for no more than nineteen hours a week, and they shared few friends between them.

They had made a powerful alliance: scientist and government minister. Skelos's achievements in neurorobotics had elevated Nylthia's parliamentary position considerably.

Nylthia did not probe Skelos about his work, although she rather admired it. She had used her influence to secure him one of the finest research facilities in Pareus and given him access to a host of prohibited technical resources.

But she balanced on the rim of the Parliamentary Elite and could only do so much. She hoped one day to sit at its centre as the new vice-chancellor. It was the highest parliamentary position any Citizen could hope to attain in the interim; the Ruling Chancellor's seat remained unfilled.

They had borne no children. Nythlia detested them. She claimed to have no recollection of her own childhood and Skelos had fancied that she been kept in a life-chamber up to the age of eighteen and then unleashed upon the world like a blizzard.

She had told him she had dissociative amnesia caused by a trauma she had suffered in her sixteenth year. He had always wondered about the trauma, so much so, he considered making her a specimen in his laboratory so that he might read her mind. But that would have been at the risk of losing her as his experiments only carried a sixty per cent chance of cognitive survival.

The Parliamentary Elite were the top tier of the Odisirian government that heralded democracy and yet ruled as a dictatorship. Skelos didn't have the time or passion for the politics to which Nylthia devoted her life.

He pecked his wife on a cheek that was as cold as her heart. She had raked her white hair up in a bun and taken most of her forehead with it. Her dark eyes were pulled upwards and outwards. Her arched brows were pulled taunt. She had angular sunken cheekbones. Her lips had been injected with a plant-based blue dye because she did not like them to lose their colour. A long billowing gown hid her willowy figure and amplified her height. Despite her coldness, men found her indifference, and her hard to read persona, attractive.

'How was your day?' The usual formality; a jumping off point for their evening conversation. Skelos always asked first as a matter of courtesy.

Like many Citizen homes, the Dorms had more space than they needed. The neutral furniture and fittings could disappear from view at the sound of a voice, a wave of the hand, a breath or a touch, receding behind panels, walls and into the floors. Chandeliers made from steel and opals hung from the ceiling. The house droids had polished the floor to such a high sheen, it resembled water in its translucency.

'Productive.' She stared out of the window, immobile. She often stood for long periods staring out at the garden view. Thinking. Planning.

Skelos summoned up a cube-shaped chair from the floor. Three floor tiles slid back, and the chair rose to take its place next to a table hewn from solid stone.

'Productive' meant that she did not have a good day. 'So how are parliamentary affairs?'

'Mundane,' she replied, 'as always. Things have not been the same since the new vice- chancellor took up the chair. I'm afraid it is not a good fit for him, even if he were slim. Sadly, there is no one to confide in. No one to trust.' She turned to him. 'How was your day?'

'A cyborg tried to kill me and I have a fool for an apprentice.'

'Oh, how is Imbrecas?' she said, brightening a little. For no reason that Skelos could fathom, she was fond of the boy.

'Among the living,' muttered Skelos, 'for now.' He brought up a holo-display from the table beside him. He scoured the food and drinks menu for a while before ordering a glass of Primnicott wine and a plate of raw fish and vegetables.

A five-legged house droid with a spherical head glided in carrying the delicacy on a tray. Controlled by voice recognition, it had no voice box of its own. Nylthia had had it modified so that it didn't make a sound. She disliked noise. She said it interrupted her thoughts and gave her headaches. Skelos had never witnessed these headaches, but according to his wife they were horrifically painful for the three seconds they lasted.

The droid set his food and drink down on the table. The sensor strip around its casing flashed blue. It then zoomed quickly away as if sensitive to the mood of the room, despite lacking the ability to detect emotions.

She nodded. 'I wanted to talk to you about Amelia.'

'She's no trouble.' *At least not for me.* Nylthia complained about Amelia daily. Every time his wife mentioned Amelia it was to make some frivolous complaint. He found it exasperating. He would have thought his wife had more demanding concerns than that of a twelve-year old girl.

'She's insolent and spoilt.'

Like any other Citizen child. 'Of course she is.' He swilled the amber-coloured wine around in his glass and devoured a sliver of fish wrapped in blue seaweed. 'You've met her mother.' Nylthia detested his wife's brother, Satcha, and yet the two women were so similar in personality and appearance they could have passed for sisters; no doubt Nylthia would disagree.

'She comes to me regularly to ask about my day. The impertinence! The events of my day should be no concern of hers. Anyone would think she were a spy. And the ribbons and the dresses are taking over the house.' She shuddered. 'Ghastly.'

'You can't blame the child, it's the mother's fault and my fool brother who married her.'

'That's why they left her in your charge to go gallivanting in Kaltharine. Smart ones. They must be mocking us as we speak.'

'I promised my brother I would take care of her, so whatever future plans you have in that calculating head of yours get rid of them.'

Nylthia took a seat at the table. 'I would never dream of parting you from your niece. I know she's very special to you despite you ranting for the first ten years of our marriage that you *don't* like children.'

'And you were ranting right alongside me and yet here she is.'

'Yes, she is here.' Nylthia gave a stiff smile. 'See to it she no longer disturbs me.'

Skelos changed the subject. 'My demonstration is tomorrow.'

'I've heard. I will be present.'

'Good. All the important Citizens will be there.'

'I should think so. Your work will catapult me up the parliamentary spectrum as to speak. And you — you my dear will have the highest accolade a scientist has ever obtained.' She gave him a rare peck on the lips.

He smiled. He liked to see Nylthia happy. Everything she said was true. Tomorrow would be a new day for them both. Their lives would change forever. Finally, the Citizens of Odisiris would acknowledge his talents. His name would be renowned. The Parliamentary Elite would elect him as an honorary member. He would head the Planetary Data Protection Committee and assume a position on the P.S.R.F.D. His name would be legend. He would shape the planet's future.

Chapter 3

Dr Skelos Dorm beamed at his audience. He held up his hand to display his blue Status Mark. He bowed to the members of the Parliamentary Elite: the vice-chancellor, Darlis Sajoyagh, and the Chief Secretary Gabe Nevassi. Potential investors and prominent members of the P.D.P.C and directors from the P.S.R.F.D made up over half the audience.

Of course, his Nylthia was there. He thought her presence would put him at ease. Instead, he found her severe expression unnerving. It was as if she had reserved it especially for him.

There were a handful of lesser known scientists present, ones who had poured scorn on his work for years. One of his former childhood friends, Osaphar Kulane, had made an appearance. Skelos did not recall inviting him, so wondered why he was there. He snorted. Well, he would show them.

The hairstylist whose services he had procured for the occasion had given his brown mane so much bounce and body it practically leapt off his shoulders with every flouncing movement he made. His black lab coat was spotless.

He had selected the theatre on the fourth floor of his Stores to carry out his demonstration. The laboratory was a hexagonal shape. Each wall was lined with rows of seats. There was a central projection screen set up on the main wall, furthest from the door. Smaller displays lined the remaining surfaces, one for each row. The hologram images from the central screen would be displayed in front of each individual seat.

The demonstration was to be conducted in the centre of the room. Skelos expected it to last more than an hour. He had allotted an extra hour for questions. He expected there would be quite a few. He had arranged drinks and some light refreshments to occupy his guests while he tripled-checked everything was in place.

'Citizens,' said Skelos, waving his hand to garner their attention. 'I thank you for your attendance. I can assure all of you that you will not be disappointed.'

He glared at his assistant, a young woman with a head of hair shaped like a tent and heavy-lidded grey eyes.

'Imbrecas would have been of more use,' Skelos hissed through his teeth. 'Do you want to put everything in place, Emphera?'

She should have been dimming the lights to emit a pale blue and cream montage, checking the subject's vitals, cleaning the tray of instruments that he had specially shipped in for ostentatious reasons. Instead, she was preoccupied with gawping at the blank central screen along with his seventeen esteemed guests.

'He's going to show us a film, isn't he?' A stiff-limbed woman in a black suit postulated to the man beside her. She was on the P.S.R.F.D board of directors. Kerss Nysen was the least impressionable amongst Skelos's audience. A sourly looking woman, broad in hips and mouth, she was known to be fastidious in her approval of scientific exploration. He had purposely planned the demonstration to coincide with her annual vacation. He had no idea why she had cancelled at the last minute.

'Why didn't he set up a communication link so we could watch it at home?' she complained. 'And what's that body doing in here?'

'Everything is in place doctor,' his assistant replied, her eyes fixed on the screen. 'Would you like some refreshments?'

Skelos gave an exasperated sigh and then clapped his hands. 'Okay. Let us begin.'

His subject, Arom Tu'ilki, lay in a padded life-chamber. Next to the life-chamber was a steel table brimming with medical supplies. Skelos was keen to show his audience that he was prepared for any eventuality and that his subjects were well cared for.

He opened the life-chamber's barrel door and checked the restraints. *Are they tight enough?* The Thruen was a willing subject and Skelos had paid him handsomely for the honour of lying in the chamber.

Half of Arom's chest was covered with markings of ancient runes native to his homeland. He was as perfect a non-Citizen specimen he was ever likely to get. He had a strong jawline, a short forehead and chin. His nose was turned up at the tip. His bulging arms lay at his sides. He had thick legs and a chiseled chest. He wore nothing but the surgical trousers his assistant had fitted him. His eyes were open because he had no eyelids. This was not a racial trait, more of a mutation. Mutants were common in the Andromeda Galaxy. The only problem was that Skelos found it hard to distinguish if Arom was unconscious, conscious, or asleep.

The Thruen was a merchant who had landed on Odisiris from his own planet of Uthren not more than two months ago. For some reason, he had not returned to his ship, and it left without him. Skelos had met him in the bar of a hotel lobby. He wouldn't have been the first Thruen who had failed to board their flight home. They were usually rounded up and deported. Arom's stay would have been short if he had not procured him for his experiments.

He took a swab from the table and swept it over Arom's upper arm. Again, this was completely unnecessary and only for show. The droid hovering close by had already sterilised his subject's arm over an hour ago. Returning to the table, he selected a prefilled electronic syringe.

'What's the matter with his eyes?' said one of the minor scientists. He rose from his seat to get a better look at Arom's face.

'Mutant. No eyelids,' whispered a man sitting behind him.

With an understanding nod, the minor scientist retreated to his chair and plucked up his glass of berry liqueur from the tray attached to his seat.

'Has he consented to this?' asked Darlis. He arched an eyebrow. The barrel-shaped Citizen, Darlis Sajoyagh, had been vice-chancellor for less than a year and behaved much like an emperor sitting on the throne of power while everyone around him made decisions on his behalf.

'Yes, he consented,' said Skelos, proffering another bow. He found the question more than a little insulting given his status and the length of his career. 'Emphera, show him the consent forms.'

Emphera duly selected a computerised tablet from a table and showed it to the Vice Chancellor. Darlis Sajoyagh rested one hand on his protruding stomach and stared briefly at the tablet.

Onas Nevassi tapped something into his own tablet. A holographic decryption tool opened above it. Skelos had no concerns there; Arom's signature was authentic.

He pumped the fluid into Arom's arm and then waved his hand in front of the Thruen's eyes. 'That should do it,' he said. He had given Arom an extra dose of anaesthetic. He didn't want him to so much as stir during the demonstration.

He turned on the apparatus and smiled at his audience. 'In a short moment, you will see a yellow light appear on the screen followed by a series of images.'

He caught the eye of Osaphar, his former friend. His stare was as cold and hard as usual. Skelos vaguely wondered if he came to offer his support, if he intended to renew their friendship. *Why else would he be here?*

Feigning indifference, he removed his gloves and pretended to read from his tablet.

'What is it you want us to see Skelos?' said Darlis Sajoyagh, postulating with his hand to the unconscious subject. He guzzled from a glass filled with blue liquid and sulphate mist. 'I don't like surprises. What is this a demonstration of?'

'The mind,' said Skelos, wringing his hands together. A bead of sweat sprung from his temple and trickled down the side of his face. A yellow light appeared on the screen. 'Ah,' he said, turning to face it.

He heard the grumbling in the audience. He gazed into the life-chamber and saw that a blood vessel had burst in Arom's eye, making the white a veiny blue. Thruens had blue blood pumping through their veins, but it was not the same colour or consistency of a blue-blooded First Status Citizen. A Thruen's blood was thinner and the blue less rich.

This wasn't good, not when he was barely fifteen minutes into his demonstration.

'Is this linked to your work in neurorobotics?' said Kerss. Arms crossed, she drummed her fingers on her forearms and glared at the yellow holographic beam hovering in front of her.

'Yes actually,' said Skelos. It had nothing to do with neurorobotics, but he didn't want to disappoint his audience. *They'll see what this is about soon enough.*

Ten minutes later, something else occurred, not as exciting as he would have hoped, more colours appeared: specks of green and blue merged with the dismal yellow light on the screen.

'What is this?' said Kerss. She batted the projected hologram with the back of her hand as if she found it offensive.

Skelos gave an embarrassed cough. He had wanted to surprise them, show them first, and then offer his superfluous explanation. 'If you could have a little patience, please.'

Thirty minutes later, Skelos heard several snores coming from the arena. Two scientists who had claimed they needed the restroom had not returned. Several of his investors were reading from their tablets. Three members of the P.D.P.C had the gall to fall asleep. The vice-chancellor appeared to be in deep conversation with Osaphar.

Emphera, his incompetent assistant, had slumped in her chair with her mouth hanging open and a control interface device in her hand. Skelos kicked her in the shin, and she woke abruptly, standing to attention and dropping the control interface on the floor.

And then it happened. The colours merged to form one giant mass. The edges of the mass grew crude stems. The stems flickered. Then they grew. The stems became like snakes, weaving themselves around the giant mass of colour. The mass then shrunk. Choked by the stems.

Arom had lifted his head from the life-chamber. The veins in his neck bulged. He gritted his teeth as if fighting to wake up from a dream.

Skelos kept a straight face. He had not seen Arom react this way when he was under before. Twice he had linked him up to the machine. He saw nothing the first time, but the second time he had seen a blurred image of Arom, sitting with his sister and brother in their home. Arom had confirmed the memory of it when he had awoken.

His gaze left Arom, and he went to the holo-display. He had not seen the image before. There was something under the mass of stems. He just couldn't make out what.

The vice-chancellor gave a weighty sigh. 'Can you explain this Skelos?'

Skelos tried his best. 'What you are seeing here is one of the subject's memories.'

'Memories?' said a member of the P.S.R.F.D. Still bleary-eyed from his nap, he was wilting in his chair with a spilled plate of canapés on his lap. 'It's a myriad of colours. Any fool can see that. And what's happened to your subject?'

Skelos looked at Arom. The Thruen made a strange gagging sound. Blood-specked foam spewed from this mouth. His skin had taken on a grey hue. The life-chamber sprung open, and his arm broke free of its restraint. It shook uncontrollably.

The image on the viewing scream began to fade; the colours die. The life-chamber alarm gave a high-pitched ring and announced to the room that the subject's vitals were failing.

Emphera stared at Skelos, a frozen expression on her face.

He hastily tried to redress the situation by adjusting the life-chamber's settings. Arom continued to convulse, tremble and wheeze for several minutes more and then he lay still. His vital signs were there on the holographic feed for all his audience to see. His vitals were fine. His brain, however, had ceased to function.

'The Thruen appears to be brain dead,' said the Chief Secretary, although this was abundantly obvious to everyone except Emphera, who pressed her hand to Arom's neck in search of a pulse.

Darlis Sajoyagh stood up. 'I think we've seen enough.'

'You think you can waste our time, Dr Dorm?' said Kerss. She threw an impatient glance in the direction of the vice-chancellor, who did not acknowledge her.

'I can assure you categorically,' said Skelos, 'the experiment works. I have conducted it on myself.'

'Then why aren't you lying in the life-chamber?' said Kerss, raising a chilled cocktail glass, filled with a frothy concoction, to her lips. 'Instead of this Thruen.'

Because I don't want you to see my thoughts. I don't want you to know what I truly am. What I'm capable of.

'I'm the only one who knows how to operate the apparatus. Arom is-was a great advocate of my work. He wanted to give his life to science—' He paused to snap at his assistant who had gathered Arom's great arm in her hands and continued to prod it for a pulse. 'Cover him up, Emphera!'

Emphera closed the life-chamber and threw a metallic sheet over it to hide his body.

'Has he family here?' asked Onas, swirling his tongue around his mouth to suck up the last remnants of the sweet pastry he had just consumed. He rubbed his hands on a napkin.

How would I blazing well know? 'No. He came alone.' He thought it was safe to assume this since he had not thought to ask Arom anything more about his family. Arom had been drunk when Skelos had met with him. Now he came to think of it, Arom had always been drunk — and angry. Skelos didn't have a clue what had spurred his anger. He couldn't have cared less. *Arom knew what he was doing when he gave his consent.*

One of the scientists who had disappeared in the restroom before his demonstration reached its horrendous climax, burst through the doors, his lab coat wafting around him. 'I have received word that a fleet of Thruens have arrived from Uthren in search of their commander-in-chief, an Arom Tu'ilki. He's missing without leave.' The scientist pointed to the life-chamber. 'They'll want an explanation.'

Skelos swallowed. Commander-in-Chief Arom had told him he was a bounty hunter. 'He lied to me,' he muttered. Not that it mattered now.

His audience filed from the room, many with their glasses in their hands, Osaphar included. A few spared him an accusatory glance; the majority didn't. The show was over, and they were moving on to the next.

Skelos gave the Chief Secretary and the vice-chancellor one final flame-faced bow.

'Let's hope his signature isn't forged Dr Dorm,' said Kerss as she rose from her chair, 'or we cannot offer you a shield to hide behind. Not that you deserve it after this farce.'

Darlis Sajoyagh addressed Kerss as she stepped from the theatre seats. 'See that all research in this facility is suspended pending an enquiry, and also see to it that the Thruen's family are informed of their loss. We won't be using any of our tech to revive him.'

Chapter 4

Skelos lay in bed trying to get the day's failings out of his mind. He had briefly drifted off to sleep when a Thruen warrior leaped out of nowhere with the biggest blade he had ever seen.

He rolled onto the floor and scuttled under the bed. He heard the ring of the blade. He heard the Thruen pad across the floor, snorting through his nose and making guttural sounds of rage. The blade slashed the bed's gossamer trim.

Skelos drew his knees up to his chest, heart pounding, hands clutched to his chest as if in prayer. He inhaled sharply through his nostrils.

Blocked by a colossal trunk stored at the top of the bed, he could go no further. He was certain that his Thruen assassin had honed and polished the blade solely for the purpose of his execution. He also suspected the assassin performed some atrocious and pointless ritual over the weapon, one that would aid in detaching his head from his body. *I wager he has a bag to put it in.*

He heard the door open. The light in the room came on. He heard his niece's voice.

'What are you doing?'

The Thruen stood up, breathing heavily. He remained at the foot of the bed. He had not come to murder a child, but Skelos feared he would take her captive to coax him out of his hiding place.

'Run Amelia,' he hissed. 'By-the-maker's-will, run!' The girl was too quick to outrun even the fastest Thruen.

'Is that you, Uncle?' said Amelia. She lifted the gossamer and peered at him.

'Tell him to come out,' said the Thruen.

'Come on,' urged Amelia. 'You must. He won't hurt us.'

Evidently, Amelia had not seen the blade.

The Thruen got over his shock of seeing Amelia. He ascertained she was not a threat and dragged Skelos from under the bed by his feet. 'You will die for what you have done. I know where to strike to ensure your instant death.'

Skelos wriggled and screeched. He imagined where the blade might strike first: his head.

Amelia squealed and ran.

'It was an accident,' he croaked. 'And he gave his consent. I have proof—' He wanted to say more, but the blade went into his back. He felt his flesh tear. He screamed and gurgled blue blood before passing out.

He woke in Nylthia's colossal bed surrounded by a sea of clothes. He felt as if he was drowning in them. He sat up and flung back the covers. His hands roamed across his back, finding only smooth skin where the wound had been. He climbed out of bed, kicking away the clothes that had tumbled to the floor when he had flung the covers away. He stretched his arms skyward. The sense of shameful failure returned. The attempt on his life paled in comparison to his catastrophic demonstration. He needed to redeem himself quickly if he wished to regain the respect and the backing of the Establishment.

Nylthia stood to one side of the bed. She had a silver gown draped over her arm. She pursed her lips and glared at him.

'Where's Amelia?' he asked.

'In her room.'

'And the Thruen?'

'Dead. He was Arom's cousin. Arom's family maintain they didn't order the attack. They said he was out of his mind with grief. They send their apologies. I had sentinels take the body away.'

Skelos nodded. 'Tell them I accept their apology and would appreciate it if you would arrange for the Planetary Data Protection Committee to increase the security around the perimeter of our home with cyborg sentinels and not the Citizen kind.'

'I shall have to move,' said Nylthia, ignoring his request.

'What are you talking about? Move where? Our home is here. The danger has passed. It was a solitary attack.'

'The failed attempt on your life has nothing to do with it. I'm sure it will be one of many. Your demonstration has caused me to rethink our relationship. My association with you after that,' she shuddered, 'fiasco could call into question my ministerial role.'

'You're my wife.'

She grimaced. 'A loose term. This is a business partnership. It always has been. What if the Parliamentary Elite think I'm involved in this Mind Work of yours. I can't have you dragging down my political career. Do you know how many years it has taken me to get this far? How many sacrifices I've had to make?'

'Yes. You remind me of them constantly. But you're my wife. We stand together. You're the most important thing, woman, in the world to me.'

'Enough of your waspish chatter. Nobody is listening and nobody cares. If you want to salvage your reputation, you'll need to see to it that your family make recompense for your disgrace in some other way. I can't do this.'

She started throwing her garments into the trunk that had been sitting under Skelos's own bed some hours ago. She called for her handmaiden, Chaijin. The handmaiden failed to heed her call. 'Where are the staff when you need them?'

One of her silk gowns hit him in the face. 'You can't leave me,' said Skelos, catching the garment in one hand and flinging it onto the bed. 'I lo-love you.' He hadn't said it for a while, and it didn't slip from his tongue as easily as it should have. But he meant it. She was his first and only love. And he didn't have the resourcefulness to find it again, not in this era.

'Don't be ridiculous. We haven't shared a bed in years. You love my status and what I can do for you. Reserve your love for Amelia and Amelia alone. I can't do any more for you, Skelos. Apart from our blood, our credibility was the only thing we had in common. I have to think about myself in these times.' She paused. 'If you want me to take Amelia for a while until you get yourself settled, I-I can. I'm going to my mother's. She can take care of her.'

'Amelia stays with me.' He collapsed onto the bed. He watched her fold her gowns in half and lay them in the trunk, her spine rigid, her face an unreadable mask. 'With your connections, you could have me reinstated, so why haven't you seen to it?'

Nylthia dispensed with folding her gowns and began tossing them into the voluminous trunk, her cheeks flaming blue. 'You know there are Citizens out there who think you're insane and then – well to have brought in a Thruen – and a high-ranking one at that. You may as well have brought in an Outsider, contaminate us all. You can't possibly believe Thruens and Citizens have the same minds, have the same thoughts. They're barbaric.'

'You're a terrible liar, Nylthia. You backed me on this. You gave me your full support.'

'I didn't fully understand your work Skelos. I never have.' She stopped packing and glared at him. 'You assured me this work was connected to neurorobotics. Either it is or it isn't.'

He ran one of her scarves' through his fingers. He hadn't trusted her enough to tell her the truth. He had been deliberately vague about the details of his Mind Work. The only Citizen who knew the full extent of his research was Denlor.

'I thought as much,' she said, whipping the scarf from his hand and tossing it into a small travel case. 'Your experiments are pointless. They don't work and once more no one cares to look inside someone's mind. Who knows what they will find.' She slammed the smallest trunk shut. 'I must think about rebuilding my reputation. You should do the same. And when you're done then perhaps, we can reunite. If it were the other way around, you would have left me. Don't deny it.'

He shrugged. He had no intention of denying it. He would have done the same if he were in Nylthia's position. It was not easy to climb the rungs of power to the Parliamentary Elite. Once you were halfway up, there would be little point in coming back down.

But he thought she would have offered him her support as a friend, as a business partner. He felt she owed him that much. He sighed. He would have to meet with his family. His indiscretions would affect all of them in the long-term.

Amelia wandered into the room, twirling the ribbon in her hair. She wore a rich indigo dress, trimmed with gemstones. She also wore her favourite pair of jewelled slippers.

Nylthia clicked her teeth. 'Move from the bed, child. Can't you see I'm trying to pack.'

Amelia stepped away from the bed. 'Are we taking a trip?' she asked, her eyes glued to the packed trunk.

'No, we are not taking a trip.' Nylthia closed her eyes. Her lips quivered.

'I'm afraid Nylthia is leaving us,' said Skelos.

Amelia turned to her uncle. 'May I have her room?'

Chapter 5

He was expelled from his Stores in front of Imbrecas and Osaphar, who once again accompanied the Parliamentary Elite members. Osaphar looked less hostile than the last time Skelos had seen him. His eyes were softer, and he offered him a rare smile. Under normal circumstances, Skelos would have greeted his invited guests with a smile, a cold, or hot beverage, and a tour.

Nervous with anticipation, he wrung his hands together. He had a large audience, many in his employ, more under the Parliamentary Elite. Kerss Nysen was among them. It didn't look good. Still he had not expected to be evicted.

The Thruen's signature had been exposed as genuine. Despite what the Thruens said, he was not at fault. He had made Arom aware of the risks before he had placed him in the life-chamber. This was a fuss about nothing. He expected the P.S.R.F.D to inspect his Stores for malpractice. And he had already seen to it that they would find nothing untoward. He knew how and when to clean up. You never knew who might drop in.

'We must ask you to leave Skelos,' said Kerss. 'Your Stores have been reallocated.'

'Reallocated?' Skelos frowned. 'All my work is here, and I've invested some of my own nano-credits in this facility. Under what law? By whose authority?'

'The vice-chancellor,' she replied. 'Do you want to speak with his secretary? I can set up a comms link now if you wish?'

Skelos felt his cheeks colouring. 'In front of my staff. Could you not have arranged a comms link in a more private setting?'

'We've had some difficulty getting hold of you.' She passed him a tablet. 'The vice-chancellor's signature.'

Skelos read the decree. The Stores were to be taken over by the Parliamentary Elite. He no longer had ownership of them. 'There is no explanation as to why here.'

'You know why. You have deviated from your work on neurorobotics. You and I both know your demonstration had nothing to do with robo-tech. The work you are undertaking is perilous.'

'I have to leave now?' he whispered. He knew it was too late to argue.

'It would be best,' she said. 'You are still under investigation.'

Kerss left with the others.

Skelos stayed behind. Those who had gathered on the balcony stayed silent.

He shouted up to them. 'Get back to work!' Some drifted back to their labs; most remained where they were. His power over them had diminished. He had lost their respect.

Fully aware of the blue tinge on his cheeks brought about by the burdening embarrassment of being extracted from the building in which he devoted his work, he lowered his gaze and he filled up a crate with several of his belongings. Only-the-Maker-knew what he was putting in it: empty containers, Oscilloscopes, bundles of wire, petri dishes. The items he no longer needed, but he thought if he kept himself busy, his audience would eventually disappear and so would the humiliation.

'Have the rest of my research apparatus sent to my house,' he told Imbrecas without looking at him. 'I'll give you a list.'

'Now?' said Imbrecas, his lips curling in disgust.

Skelos felt so light-headed, he thought he might faint. 'No, when I get home. You may leave now.'

When he looked up, he found Osaphar watching him. *Not again. Why must he always catch me at my worse?* He barked at him. 'Why are you still here?'

'I did try to stop them. I want you to know that,' said Osaphar. 'You could appeal.'

The two of them were alone for the first time in years. Skelos recalled their childhood friendship. It was one of the happiest times in his life. *When had other things got in the way?* He sighed, remembering. It was after their visit to the Red Caves. That's when everything changed, or at least, that's when he did.

Skelos wanted to tell him to stop with the pretence. Of course, he could appeal, but no one would listen. Instead he said, 'If that's what you say, then that's what I believe.'

'I still don't understand what you hoped to achieve. Nylthia was keen that I should attend.'

He was surprised that Nylthia would have her hand in something so personal. 'I thought you were there at the vice-chancellor's invitation. I noticed that the two of you have become quite friendly.'

Osaphar gazed up at the balconies. 'I want to talk with you in private.'

Skelos took him to his private room. The one in which he had kept the young Outsider.

'What do you want to tell me?' said Skelos, once the door had shut behind them.

'I'm no friend of Darlis Sajoyagh,' said Osaphar. 'On the contrary, I believe he may be an enemy. Therefore, I think it wise that I keep him close.'

'Then I admire you. If I kept all my enemies close, I'd choke them and I doubt if I'll have *any* friends who will save me from the consequences of my actions.' His tone was more cutting than he intended.

Osaphar moved closer to him. He dug his fingers into Skelos's arm. 'We're in danger.'

Skelos retched free from him. 'Don't be so melodramatic.'

'An assassin tried to kill me, not three nights ago. A Thruen. I killed him first.'

'Oh, that danger,' said Skelos, recounting his own near-death escape from the previous night. Were the Thruens so enraged over Arom's death they wanted to murder all who witnessed his demonstration? It seemed an unlikely coincidence, but not an implausible one. Someone had attempted to take his life, not once, but twice if he counted the cyborg.

'And the attempted murder weapon?'

'A Tauk'lr blade.'

Tauk'lr blades were infused with poison, but not one strong enough to kill a Citizen; their cells regenerated too quickly. *If the Thruen were a true assassin, he would have known this.*

'Perhaps he only meant to scare you. Do you know of anyone else who was present at my demonstration who this assassin attacked?'

'What has an attempt on my life got to do with your demonstration?' Osaphar placed a card, forged from titanium alloy, into Skelos's hand.

It was a Datas card, held by the members of the Parliamentary Elite. 'He had this on him.'

'Do you know whose it is?' Skelos's thoughts flew to Nylthia before he could stop them. Stalking the room, his arms folded. The humiliation had left him. He was over it. *Now I think of it, I shall appeal.* 'I hope you're not suggesting it was Nylthia.' He was eager to dispense with any impending suggestions she was involved. Although the likelihood of it being Nylthia was absurd. She had always held a fondness for Osaphar and the entire House of Kulane.

'I think it has something to do with Eron. About what he entrusted to us.'

Skelos laughed. His friendship with the former Ruling Chancellor of Odisiris had ended many years before his death. 'He never entrusted me with anything. By the Palm-of-My-Maker, it's preposterous. You have been—'

'What about the tablet he gave you? The one he gave to each of us and told us never to lose sight of.'

Skelos had lost sight of his when he threw it out of an airship window and into the lake below. He wondered if it was still there intact. He had transferred the encrypted data on to a file and then forgotten all about it.

It wouldn't have been the first time Eron had given him something for safe-keeping that turned out to be inconsequential drivel. He had given him the tablet when he was thirteen-years old. Their friendship ended three years later, and Eron never asked for it back. Skelos couldn't think why the Parliamentary Elite would be interested in the files after all these years.

'I no longer have the files,' said Skelos. 'And you?'

Osaphar shook his head 'Mine were destroyed in the fires. You remember.'

Oh, yes, the fires. Years ago, the summer fires reached the Pareus perimeter and destroyed many homes, Osaphar's among them.

'I wonder now what was on it.'

'It doesn't matter to us what was on it. It matters to someone in the Parliamentary Elite. Don't share what I have told you with Nylthia.'

Skelos nodded. Evidently, Osaphar hadn't heard that his wife had walked out on him.

After Osaphar had left, Skelos packed up all he could carry. That night he went to the city vaults to retrieve the encrypted file. It was not there. There was no indication that the vault had been broken into. He could have taken it out, misplaced elsewhere. He was too tired to do a more thorough search. It was late, and he was desperate to lay his head on a pillow for the night — assassin or no assassin.

Chapter 6

Skelos trudged through the front door, weary from a long day. The inviting aroma of sizzling meat and simmering roots greeted him. He leaned down to remove boots. He was eager to put his aching feet up.

As soon as his boots were discarded. He sank into the couch's soft cushions with relief.

A circular dining table rose from the floor, and a droid laid the plate of food before him: *roruck* meat, charred on the outside and still pink within, a quivering pile of fish eggs, and green roots, all courtesy of his efficient chef droid. He snatched up his fork and speared one of the roruck haunches, fat and juicy. As he lifted it to his mouth, its deep purple blood dripping down his chin. He enjoyed his meat rare. He summoned the droid for some wine. After the day's events, he needed a strong drink.

Amelia stared out of the window that looked on to the gardens, just as Nylthia had once done. He wondered if she secretly missed her. 'How was your day, Uncle?' she said, turning from the window.

She is mocking me. Mocking my memory of Nylthia. He wanted to get the woman out of his mind. He had closed his heart to her as soon as she stepped out of the door. Sentiment and emotion would tear him apart and take him down a path from which there was no return. Despair was not tolerated in the House of Dorm.

'Move from the window, Amelia. Move away at once!'

The girl stepped away from the window. She wore a violet dress. The skirt of the dress made her look as if she were midway up a hill. And the bow on the neckline was so large, it almost eclipsed her face.

'Is that the manner in which you greet me?' he snapped.

'No, Uncle. Sorry. I'm pleased to see you, Uncle.' She gave a courtesy and sat down.

'That's better.' He wiped the meat juice from his lips with his napkin.

Amelia watched him eat. He found her stare unbearable. She obviously had something to say.

He was starting to lose his appetite. He gazed at her.

'What did you want to say, Amelia?'

'I was wondering what happened to my parents.'

'They're on Kaltharine where they have been for the past four months.' He couldn't stop thinking about the encrypted file Eron had given him and why he had entrusted him with it.

'Not them. My real parents.'

He dropped his fork. *Why is she bringing this to me now? While I have this whole retched assassin business to contend with?* 'What are you talking about?' He dare not look at her despite the fact her expression remained unchanged. She seldom smiled or cried, but she did laugh, often at things he didn't find amusing.

'Mother told me yesterday. She said that she and father adopted me after my real parents abandoned me.'

Satcha was a cunning woman; he'd give her that. She must have relished telling Amelia that he had not given birth to her. Her motives were clear. She wanted to make her his responsibility and chastise him for discrediting the House of Dorm name she had married into.

'I don't know anything about your real parents. It was a closed adoption. You shouldn't dwell on it.'

He didn't want Amelia to know he was the one who had found her on his doorstep, and he had caught a glimpse of the man who had left her there. He was too dumbfounded to go after him. Reluctant to take on the burden of a child, he had given her to his brother, Aughen, who at the time had been thinking of starting a family. Aughen had a son from his previous marriage, but he had borne no children with Satcha.

Aughen had tracked down Amelia's real father, a First Status Citizen from the city of Whirim.

The child's mother was dead. The father was wanted for murder and had been exiled shortly after. The details of his crime remained a mystery.

Aughen had kept the details of whatever arrangement he had made with the girl's fugitive father to himself. And there had to have been some arrangement as the adoption was never official, and her abandonment was never made public.

'Is it true they abandoned me?' she asked. 'Mother said, you asked them to take me, that you were the one who found me. Is that true?'

He thought about denying it, but he wanted Amelia to trust him when nobody else did.

'It's true,' he said. 'They abandoned you. I was too busy to give you the attention you required, and my brother and sister-in-law can't have children—'

'But father has a son, doesn't he? There's a picture of him in their flower garden.'

Curse Satcha and her vengefulness. He had forgotten about that one picture in the flower garden. 'He's gone. They hardly speak of him.' This was true. Aughen hadn't spoken to his son in eight years; hadn't seen him in two. 'Don't tell me you want to go looking for them because we haven't the time or the workforce.'

'I don't want to find them. My life is in the palm of the Maker. What is to become of us, Uncle?'

Skelos helped himself to a drink from the cabinet. *What is to become of me?* Experiments were not always successful on the first attempt and before a live audience when one's nerves were frayed. He would use theses excuses to form the basis of his appeal. There was no harm in trying. It was better than drinking himself into a stupor every night.

'Uncle?'

'You needn't worry, Amelia.'

'Mother and father haven't called today.' She gulped. 'And they didn't call yesterday.'

He gazed at her. She had taken his seat on the couch. *Is she going to cry?*

To appease the child, Skelos contacted his brother. He knew Aughen's lack of contact had nothing to do with the child and everything to do with his failed demonstration and the unfortunate Thruen. His brother was always cautious in matters that might be detrimental to the family name.

Aughen and Satcha appeared on the holo-display dressed in matching blue tunics. His brother's shoulders were as broad as the back of the chair in which he sat. Satcha sat so close to her husband their hair was entangled, his brother's coarse locks with his wife's spikey mane. The Kaltharine sun had turned Satcha's skin a mottled blue.

'We heard what happened...oh, hello, Amelia,' said Aughen.

'Hello, Father,' said Amelia. 'Hello, Mother. How are you?'

'Very well, my treasure,' said Satcha, flashing her jagged teeth. She looked at Skelos, her eyes narrowing.

'I think we should have this conversation in private,' said Aughen.

Skelos sent Amelia away.

'It was obviously an accident,' said Skelos, after she had gone. 'The nature of the job.'

Satcha grimaced and sighed.

He didn't want to give Satcha the satisfaction of knowing that she had angered him by telling Amelia about her adoption.

'Rent Stores outside the city and continue your neurorobotics work there,' Aughen advised. 'Regain the Establishment's trust.'

'I tire of such work.'

'Don't you understand the implications of what you have done? The Parliamentary Elite see you as a threat. It is one thing to create cybernetic organisms with Citizen DNA and quite another to try to delve into the workings of a Citizen's mind, to read it. Such exploration is dangerous and could be misinterpreted. Some believe that you are plotting against the government.'

'That's absurd,' said Skelos. 'I have no reason to plot against anyone.' *But given time...*

'What you think doesn't matter,' said Aughen. 'It's what *they* think.'

Chapter 7

Skelos had been dreaming about the time he spent in the Red Caves as a child; a time when he, Osaphar, and Eron were still friends, when he sensed there was someone or something in the room with him. He felt a chill on his leg. He jerked it back under the covers with a start, only to be dragged down to the floor. He thrashed his arms about in the semi-darkness. He didn't cry out at first; part of his brain was still locked in the dream.

The sharp barb that sprung from the droid's head missed Skelos's own and struck him in the shoulder. He had spun away at just the right moment. A barb to the head may have been the end for him.

He gave a yelp of pain as the barb pierced his shoulder. He slammed open the door to the balcony and leapt over the wall. The droid followed, zipping through the air, its barb whirring angrily. He ran quite some distance in his nightwear, yelling with hysteria, until he calmed down, came to his senses and realised he had control of the droid. He closed his eyes for one split second, seized the droid with one hand and slammed it into the ground. It died as only droids can die, with a spark, a screech and a hiss.

That was close. Too close. The Thruens were getting better. He rushed back into the house and immediately went to check on Amelia. He discovered she had slept through the whole ordeal.

He contacted a company called Secure Homes and asked them to provide high-grade sentinel cyborgs: the type that were difficult to hijack. He then contacted Nylthia via a visual link and informed her of the threat.

'We'll step up our enquiries,' she advised him. 'And I shall see to it you have every protection.' She then signed off without saying any more.

Skelos accessed the surveillance records from the previous night. He saw no one enter, but he did see a house droid drift into the gardens overlooking the living room area and reappear an hour later. He could have sworn he saw a shadow by the trees. He replayed the footage over and over again until his head hurt and he no longer knew what he was seeing. The shadow became a branch, and then the moon, and then nothing.

He took the house droid apart. It was fitted with a tiny tracking device, which could have caused the droid to malfunction. He checked the other two house droids. He found no irregularities in either of them.

By mid-morning he had put the attack on his life to the back of his mind. He thought about what his brother had said. He trusted his word. He should try to regain the Establishment's faith. He considered renting Stores outside the city.

A droid brought him some warm bread, its mechanical movements betraying no emotion. It wasn't until he had finished eating it that he noticed Amelia had not appeared for breakfast. She usually rose before him.

He went to look for her. She was not in her room. He strode into the gardens and visited the glass bench where she often sat. He found it bare. His heart started to beat a little faster. His throat tightened. He dropped onto the glass bench trying to catch his breath. He tried to call Amelia's name, but in the throes of his panic attack he only managed rasping breaths. His sixth sense told him she was gone. He clutched his hand to his chest to quell his palpitations. He stalked inside and opened the drinks cabinet. He downed half a bottle of Primnicott. He felt the world collapse around him, his Status fading.

Could she have gone to see his brother and sister-in-law? *I should have let her talk to them a while longer before sending her to bed.*

He called Osaphar and told him of Amelia's disappearance. He arrived within the hour.

'I warned you,' said Osaphar, the moment he stepped through the door. 'Did you not take any of the precautionary measures I advised?'

Skelos led him into the living room. 'There is no trace of her on the Nano databank.'

All Citizens had a nano-chip inserted under their skin, six weeks after birth. But if the nano-chip was faulty or had been tampered with, it didn't always show up on the databank.

Skelos helped himself to glass of Primnicott and offered one to Osaphar, which he declined. 'This hasn't anything to do with the conspiracy theories of yesteryear. She may have run away.' He stared out of the window at the glass bench. An aerial drone had skimmed over the garden. He thought about sending it out again – to be certain.

'Then why call me?'

'I didn't know who else to call.'

Osaphar raised his eyebrows. 'Her parents?'

'Don't be ridiculous. We must find her first. She can't have gone far. I've sent out an aerial drone and the sentinels are on alert. If someone had abducted her, we would have received some communication from her captors by now.' He glugged down his glass of wine. 'Can you not sit? You're making me nervous.'

Osaphar leaned against the wall, his arms folded. 'I think you're doing that all by yourself. I'll get a search party organised. You should lay off the drink. You need to stay alert.'

'Yes, yes,' he set his glass down. 'Be discreet.'

'I think you should leave here.'

Can he make no practical suggestions? 'No. They have my Stores. They cannot have my home as well. Besides, Amelia will not know where to look if I were to leave now.' He poured himself another glass of wine and stared out of the window as he sipped it.

Osaphar left without saying goodbye. Skelos failed to notice. He spent two long hours gazing out of the window before grabbing a half-finished bottle of Primnicott and sinking into his chair. After a few swigs from the bottle, he fell fast asleep.

He had the most vicious nightmares. The Thruens attacked him in his bed, slashing at him with spears and long knives. Like savages. This nightmare was followed by an army of cyborgs who shot him at Nylthia's command.

He woke in a cold sweat. The near empty bottle of Primnicott rolled off his lap and smashed to the floor. He scrambled up and grabbed his father's Bolt-Shot Whip from a cabinet on the wall. Then in the eerie silence, he patrolled the great house, vowing to stay awake in case anyone or anything came in or out of it.

Chapter 8

Two days had passed, and Amelia had not been found. As Osaphar had said it would be a discreet operation. So discreet was it, in fact, Skelos questioned whether a search *was* being conducted. Finding her should not have been an issue. However, if her disappearance were to be made public, it would bring him enough unwarranted attention, and he had enough to last him a lifetime. He could only imagine the burgeoning of his brother's wrath if he learned of his daughter's disappearance, in light of his catastrophic demonstration.

He has spent the past two nights wrapped up in his woes, sleeping on a chair. His supply of Primnicott was running dry, and he turned to his beloved Zaskian with a price tag so high that every sip was bittersweet.

He heaved himself from the chair and stretched his arms above his head. He glanced at the window. And there he saw her, sitting on the glass bench with her hands in her lap. She wore a silk crepe dress and a rose garland headband. Skelos opened the patio doors in haste, afraid that he was in some half-crazed dream. He lunged at Amelia, pulling her to his chest in a tight, almost manic embrace. Yes, it was her. She was real. He let her go. She moved past him, staring ahead of her. He followed her gaze. She was looking at the arched Pylori tree with its thick green buds and flagella blowing in the light morning breeze. Its bows were heavy with dark fruit.

Is this a trap? Is another assassin waiting in the gardens for me?

'Amelia,' he grabbed her shoulders and pivoted her in his direction. 'What happened to you?'

'Nothing. I've been here.'

'You can't have been here. You've been missing for two days. What do you remember?'

'I remember going for a walk in the gardens and sitting on this bench, and then, I think I saw a ghost. Yes, that was it, Uncle. I saw a ghost.'

'A ghost? Where did you learn that word?' Ghosts did not exist, nor more so than the Maker. Such words had been created to annotate the unexplained; they carried no true meaning.

'I don't know.'

'Did this-this ghost ask you for something?'

'It asked me if I lived here?'

'That was all?'

'There might have been more. I don't remember.'

He ushered the child inside. *My enemies are trying to bludgeon me with fear.* Ghosts were things of myth and legend, often aligned with other worlds, but not their world. Amelia's captors must have modified her mind. It was the only explanation. He was certain of it. They had planted the 'ghost' in her head to make her forget the events leading up to her abduction. He didn't want another night of uninvited guests in his home.

That night he took Amelia to a Secure Homes safe house and returned home alone. He informed Osaphar of Amelia's unexplained return and instructed him to call off the search.

He went out into the garden and sat where she sat, on the glass bench that looked on to the Pylori tree. He sat there for close to an hour before he saw it. It wasn't the tree she had been looking at, he realised. It was the glasshouse behind the tree. He had only ever entered it twice. It was where Nylthia grew her exotic and sometimes deadly plants. He hastened to the glass house armed with his Bolt-Shot Whip, and an extendable metal rod, good enough to knock someone off their feet if they were to catch him up.

The interior of the glasshouse was hot and sticky. Someone had shut the skylight.

Nylthia harboured a large collection of the *Opis* plant. Its stringy purple tentacles were poisonous if digested. The release of poison was slow, too slow to kill a Citizen. There were orange flowers and blue bulbs that had not yet opened. Some of the plants grew in small life-chambers, others were in modified pots that gave them all the nourishment and artificial sunlight they needed. One of the plant life-chambers had been smashed.

Someone had been in here, but not recently. The smashed plant had withered. Its green liquid seeped across the floor, and it produced a putrid odour.

Is this where Amelia met her captor?

As he waded deeper into the glass house, he noticed more evidence of an intruder: smashed and empty life-chambers, decomposing plants.

He found the wireless remote for the Gunan pod on the floor. He usually kept it inside his bedchamber cabinet. He clucked with annoyance. He had seen Amelia playing with the remote not more than two months ago. He had told her to return it to where she had found it. He picked up the device and stared around, slapping the remote against the palm of his hand. It could be that Amelia's captors set her free when they learned the identity of their intended target. They must have assumed the risk of abducting her, in order to secure a ransom, was too great and returned her to the garden.

He went inside.

He ventured to his bedchamber and brought up the Gunan pod from beneath the floor. The floor panel slid back. The white egg-shaped pod rose on its dusty lectern. The antique from his youth had been in his home for as long as he could remember. He swept his hand over the pod's centre and the door popped open. He stepped inside.

Her beauty mesmerised him. He had once harboured some sort of love for her. But the relationship would never work out. He touched her face and his hand went through her cheek: a solid holographic imprint. Who knew where her true home lay. All he knew was she never left her pod. He used to visit her almost every day as a child, but in adolescence he outgrew her. As he focused on his desire to become a scientist, she became a child's toy and a dream. And she became an ancient heirloom forever bound to the House of Dorm. He believed her to be a cybernetic machine; a sophisticated memory bank. She certainly acted like one. She never blinked. Her hands sat frozen in her lap and she was dead behind the eyes. She seldom spoke. When she did she rarely made any sense, and her words were not directed at him.

She said she came from the planet Gunan in the Andromeda Galaxy. The tiny planet had a population of less than two million Citizens. It had been destroyed many years ago by a thermonuclear blast. Some of the people who dwelled there fled to other planets within the galaxy, but most perished. Skelos liked to fancy that the woman, who he named Orel, was one of the survivors. Although he had never been able to find her. She had a mark on the palm of her left hand unlike his own. It was a symbol made up of circles and squares.

He knelt at the foot of the chair inside the cramped pod. He left the door ajar to let in some air. 'How are you, Orel? My apologies for not coming sooner. I was busy – as it happens – with life. I'm a scientist now, though others would question it. I have got myself into some difficulty, Orel. My career is all but ruined. Those who are eager to supplant me shall make it so. There are assassins out there,' he pointed to the open door, 'trying to kill me.'

'Fortification,' said Orel.

It wasn't the first time she had said that word. He had no idea what she meant. When he asked her, he received no reply.

'We haven't spoken in years and you can think of nothing more to say?' He sighed. There were no projectors inside the pod or the remote device that could account for the hologram.

He rose from the floor and sat on the chair, slipping through her transparency.

'I don't want to give up, Orel. I won't let the Establishment crush me. Any words of wisdom?' He paused. Hopeful. He thought that in the twenty-one years since his last visit, she may have learned an extra word or two. 'I guess not then,' he said after several minutes had passed.

He slammed his eyes shut. The chair was comfortable. It was a shame it was rooted to the floor.

He fell asleep. He dreamt that Orel was real and that they lay together in the glass house. Caught within the dream threads, he felt his body growing hot. The heat drew him from his sleep. He opened his eyes. The pod door was shut. He kicked it open with his foot. He jumped up from the chair and spun round. She was gone. She had never disappeared from her chair in all the years he had visited her. He ran his hand under the chair in search of a power source. It wasn't something he hadn't done a thousand times before. *Must everything be taken from me?* He left the pod, slamming the door shut.

That night he slept in the house, for the first time in years, with no other Citizens for company. He had sentinel cyborgs posted at every entrance and exit and a tracker drone at the door. He lay on top of his bed too discontent and hot to climb under the covers. He noticed Orel was standing in the corner of the room, steeped in shadow and mystery. He swept his hand across the table on his wall to put on his night-light, afraid that if he used voice recognition, the noise would make her disappear.

She was still there. He climbed out of bed. He touched her face; his hand went straight through her cheek. *Not real.* But she seemed more real outside the pod than in. She had a long torso and a tiny waist. She did not blink, but her face looked as if it had shifted him some way. Her lips looked softer and eyelids more prominent. It was a slight shift, but it was there.

A hologram was not an entity. It did not move of its own free will. Someone was still controlling it after all these years, or they had only just started to control it again. Although as far as he could tell the hologram no longer held any real purpose than to amuse and torment him. He ran his hand across his mouth thoughtfully. Perhaps the real 'Orel' had created a droid in her form to act as some sort of decoy.

'What made you leave your chair, Orel, after all these years?'

'Fortification.'

'Yes, we know fortification. What else? What else are you not telling me?'

He switched on the holographic table and pulled the Gunan files from Vega's virtual database. The planet was destroyed by a meteorite. He flicked through the profiles of the known survivors. There were many, but none of them matched Orel's description. His eyes ached. Hadn't he checked these records two decades ago? He had not learnt anything then, and nothing would have changed since. *No. This won't work.*

'Fortification.' He muttered the word under his breath several times. He saw that Orel had moved again. She stood at the foot of his bed of all places. *Now this is getting sinister.* He couldn't undress in front of her, never mind sleep.

'Index Eleven,' she said.

This is new information. Words she had never uttered before.

Index Eleven? There were no constituencies in Gunan, only districts and none of them had an eleventh index. If Orel wasn't standing in front of him like some immobile spectre from his dreams, he may have allowed himself to forget about her.

The thought of her moving about his home gave him cause for concern. Was this the ghost to which Amelia had referred? He knew he had the ability to make her disappear, to zap her where she stood, but then she would disappear from his life forever and he was not ready to lose her, especially when he had lost so much already.

He entered the kitchen. He took Osaphar's advice and poured himself a glass of water as opposed to wine. He put on some relaxing music. *The Establishment can't get me to move, but that damned Orel just might.* He hummed along to the rhythm, closed his eyes and swayed. The music stopped abruptly. He opened his eyes. Orel stood not an inch from his face, her eyes cemented to his. He dropped his glass.

A house droid zoomed into view. Skelos stepped out of its way to allow it to do its work: mopping up the water and depositing the broken glass into its outer bin dispenser.

This is all too much. He called Denlor.

He had never seen Denlor grin so widely as when he saw Orel's hologram. Denlor had spent three years studying holography, dedicating much of his research to hologram classifications and illumination techniques.

'She follows me everywhere,' said Skelos.

Denlor crossed his arms. 'Even to your bed. That's what you want, isn't it?'

'It's not what I want. And don't you dare tell anyone about this. It's not what you think. It's been here since my childhood, and now for some bizarre reason it has started moving around the house.'

'Have you looked for a holographic port?'

Skelos slapped his hand to his forehead. 'Now why didn't I think of that? There is no holographic port,' he hissed.

'There's always a holographic port. Show me where you found her.'

Skelos took him to his bedchamber, and the smile disappeared from Denlor's face. 'You found her in a hydro-pod and you never reported it?'

'Me? I was an infatuated child. I don't know if my parents ever reported it. I never discussed it with them, and they never discussed it with me.'

Orel reappeared in a corner of the bedchamber.

'Well, you really are a master of secrets, aren't you, doctor?'

Denlor stepped inside the pod. He ran his hands over the walls and the chair. 'I'm surprised you didn't take it apart.' He took out a small disc and placed it on the chair. It made a beeping sound.

'I couldn't detect any laser apparatus,' said Skelos. 'I assume it's being controlled outside a visible range.'

Denlor picked up the device. 'There's no holographic port inside the pod. Did you open it up in here?'

'Yes.'

'I mean the first time?'

'Yes.'

'Did it say anything to you?'

'Nothing that made any sense. I know the pod came from Gunan. Have you ever heard of Index Eleven?'

'No. Anything else?'

'It wants protection. It keeps saying fortification.'

'I don't think it's asking for protection.'

'If fortification is not asking for protection, then what is?'

'Fortification is a planet.'

Skelos watched Denlor flush with pleasure at announcing something that he had clearly misinterpreted. 'Impossible. There are no known unidentified planets within the Andromeda galaxy.' He had never claimed to be an astronomer, but if a planet had a name, Vega would have a record of it.

'That's the thing Fortification isn't in the Andromeda galaxy.' Denlor took the holographic detector out of the pod and laid it on the table. It went off. 'Looks as if it's inside your walls.'

Chapter 9

Well, that was one mystery solved. Skelos had never thought to look for the holographic projector elsewhere. He was so embarrassed by his lack of foresight regarding its detection, he quickly steered Denlor back to the subject of Fortification.

'Fortification lies within the Messier Galaxy,' said Denlor. 'It's tiny, has a population of about 50,000 Denizen hybrids with racial traits similar to our own. You, like many other Citizens, have spent years studying the Andromeda Galaxy. You forget about the others.'

'And how come you know about it?'

'I worked in the landing port lounges when I was younger. A couple of ships from the Messier Galaxy docked for repairs, refuelling, that sort of thing.'

'I didn't know ships from other galaxies were allowed to dock on Odisiris. I thought it was against Establishment policy.

'I believe they were in desperate need.' Denlor helped himself to a drink without being offered one. If it were anyone else, Skelos would have taken the glass from them and told them to leave.

'You say you witnessed two ships dock?'

'Only two ships from the Messier Galaxy have ever docked on Odisiris. Three years apart. None since.' Denlor sat down on a chair, rocking the glass in his hand.

'Did any of the crew ever leave the docking port?'

'Now that is one thing we know the Establishment would never allow, but it doesn't mean it's not possible.'

'She could be here.' *This thing of beauty.*

Denlor sighed. 'Considerably older, I would imagine.'

'Not if she's a cybernetic organism.' *Her beauty will be everlasting.* 'Can you get me a list of all those on board?'

Denlor retrieved the classified manifests from the Vega database.

There were two-hundred-twenty names in all. More than Skelos had expected. The crew on *The Zakota* numbered just twenty-two, the rest were on the *Luskel Suix*.

Skelos examined the crew member's profiles.

'I'll leave you with these,' said Denlor. 'Make sure you go offline within one hour or you could trigger an unauthorised access tracker. 'Why bother looking into this?' He said as he was leaving. 'It's meaningless.'

'Nothing is meaningless,' he informed Denlor. 'Besides, I need to take my mind off the investigation.'

Skelos overrode the unauthorised access tracker and returned to perusing the profiles of all two-hundred-twenty names in *The Zakota* and *Luskel Suix* manifests. After three hours of searching, he found her: Lieutenant Elise Fisher of *The Zakota*, aged thirty-four.

The Zakota was the last ship from the Messier Galaxy to arrive on Odisiris all those years ago. If she had stayed in Odisiris she could have changed her identity. If she were a lieutenant she may have joined the fleet, which meant she could be anywhere.

He searched for Index Eleven, Fortification. He found no constituencies, only more districts, towns and cities.

He considered asking Nylthia about the hydro-pod. He chose his mother instead. She was the closest to him. She denied knowing anything about the Gunan pod as he suspected she would. But he could see the troubled look in her eye when she asked him if it was empty.

'It was,' he told her. 'I'm just clearing out.'

He called Secure Homes to check on Amelia before he retired for the night. He couldn't allow her to return with a hologram-spectre drifting about the house.

He drank himself to sleep. Hours later, he woke cradling an empty bottle of Zaskian and a sea-crab claw. Two pairs of eyes watched him. One set belonged to Orel, the other to Elise.

Chapter 10

The woman had Orel's eyes. Nothing more. She had lost her figure. She had once been beautiful, but the harshness of life must have made her age prematurely. She had lines on her face. Too many for a woman that, by his calculation, could not have been older than fifty-five. She was not the 'Orel' hologram he had seen in the Gunan pod, that was someone or something else.

Elise wore a tatty brown cloak and a long tunic made of hemp from a bygone era. Her hair was wiry and ruffled. Her nails were worn down to the tip. She looked like an Outsider: bedraggled and lost.

'Please come with me,' she said.

Inquisitive, he followed her without asking how she got into his home. She had docked a small, dented warship next to one of his air shuttles.

The warship ramp-way lowered, and they went inside.

Elise piloted the ship. Its ascent was smooth.

For the longest time, Skelos sat in the co-pilot's chair, watching the way her eyes scanned the horizon that held him, the way they searched the empty blue as if looking for something just out of reach. She left the cockpit, leaving the ship on auto-pilot. She returned shortly after with a cup in her hands. She handed it to him. 'You look as if you need it.'

He took the cup from her. It contained a hot brew made from a bitter plant called *Hyis*. It was known to soothe headaches and rehydrate the body. He sipped it slowly. Its sharpness brought him some clarity. He had left his home in favour of the fathomless blue skies and beyond. 'Where are you taking me?'

She eased herself back into the pilot seat, her eyes on him. 'Nowhere. We're just circling.'

'I've been searching for you, lieutenant. Where have you been all this time?'

'Brevons Beach.'

He nodded. It explained her shabby appearance. Brevons Beach stripped you of all wealth and dignity, if you ever had any to begin with.

'I don't think it's safe we land there, do you?' If they landed on Brevons Beach, he would never see Pareus again. He would be ransomed off to the highest buyer or, worse, killed. 'Are you abducting me?'

'No.'

'But you abducted my niece and wiped her memory.'

'I'm sorry about that. We had to be certain that our mission had not been comprised, that the House of Dorm residency had not changed hands since I was last there. I left the hydro-pod behind when I landed. I'm from Gunan, but I grew up on Fortification. It was very hard for me to get out here and explain myself. The part-humanoid malfunctions. You received her message?'

So he was right about Orel. She was only part-human. *An enigma.* 'All she tells me is that she comes from Gunan. She also says the words Fortification and Index Eleven.'

She pulled her ragged cloak around her. 'That's it? She says nothing more?'

'No. Is she supposed to?'

She pinched her lips, frowning. 'But you must have received the message. The signal went out.'

'What signal?'

'I received a signal from Fortification. The people were readying themselves for war.'

The poor woman was confused, and who could blame her, surviving on Brevons Beach for so long with mercenaries and other Citizen degenerates. He patted her hand. 'How terrible to be thwarted with such delusions.'

Elise stared at his hand before gently brushing it away. 'I don't think you understand. I've been trying to get the part-humanoid to deliver the message to you for years. The time has finally come. The revolutionists are moving to overthrow President Tusan, our leader on Fortification. They have been patiently planning the coup for years. We have formed an alliance with a group of Higher Citizens from your planet, dedicated to the cause. They said they will help us in our time of need. That time has now come. You are doctor Skelos Dorm, are you not? Your House was on the list of trusted Citizens when the message was delivered. You need to contact Zatar, using the encrypted gateway 351310. He has organised the guerrilla forces. Can you tell me of your plans?'

Skelos gawped at her. Evidently, she was deranged. *Don't panic.* Nylthia had dealt with these types in the past. They had never gotten further than their front gates. 'I don't share my plans with the messenger. Now do you want to drop me back home.'

'Forgive me,' she said, bowing her head. 'You must want to speak with the part-humanoid. She is on board.'

Skelos followed her to the crew's quarters. When the door slid back, he saw Orel sitting on one of the bunks with her hands resting in her lap. She had not changed. There was something strangely ethereal about her.

I am in love. 'She has not aged,' he said.

'She is my twin sister, was, I suppose. Her name is Tabiatha. Very little of her is humanoid now: a leg and a small segment of her brain, but to call her a cyborg would be an insult.'

He nodded. *Interesting.* He had never met a part-humanoid: those who had parts of their body replaced by machinery due to disease or injury. Citizens had the ability to self-heal, which was not always the case with Denizen hybrids.

Elise spoke to her sister. 'Deliver your message regarding Index Eleven.'

'My name is Tabiatha. I am from planet Gunan. I currently reside on the planet Fortification, located within the Messier Galaxy. I want to tell you about Index Eleven. Index Eleven is a list of planets compiled by a select group of revolutionists from planets wishing to overthrow their leaders in the hopes of replacing them with a new order. Gunan was not destroyed by a meteorite but by a nuclear explosion commanded by vice-chancellor Ceroh of Kaltharine. Your former Ruling Chancellor was murdered by a member of your own Parliamentary Elite, Onas Pralyeton. Please contact Zatar to strategise your plans. We await your signal.'

So this explained it. Skelos sunk into the chair and drew a few shuddering breaths. It was hard to believe the Ruling Chancellor, his childhood friend had been murdered. 'But I didn't send a signal.'

'Your wife then or the child?' said Elise.

Skelos shook his head. How could he send a signal? When he never understood the message.

His heart leapt at the sound of gunfire. The ship rocked under the impact. It was coming from behind them. A ship was in pursuit. Some distance away, it resembled a feathered silver halo.

Elise inspected the ship's rear navigation screen. She tapped some of the controls. Her warship dipped and then released its loaded missiles directly into the nose of the pursuing vessel. It exploded in a ball of white and yellow flames.

She then took the warship higher. The clouds rushed up to meet them, and for a moment, the world vanished in a shroud of white.

Skelos's ears throbbed as pressure built inside his head. His breaths grew shallow while the cockpit air grew thin. He looked around for an oxygen mask but couldn't see one. 'I didn't send the message. Take me home.'

'I can't—'

He would have had to be out of his mind to let Elise launch them into outer space in a corroding vessel. 'Take me home now!'

When the ship docked outside his home, he scrambled down the ramp-way before it had fully lowered, eager to feel land under his feet once more. His blocked ears deadened all sound. Though it was cool outside, sweat soaked through his clothing.

He hurried inside without bidding Elise goodbye.

He secured the door behind him. Alone at last, he refilled his glass from the near-empty bottle on the counter. As the liquid splashed over the rim, his hand began to shake. The glass slipped from his grasp and shattered on the floor. He stared at the mess. *No more drink.* He needed to keep his wits about him. Maintain his sanity.

He wiped his mouth, tasting the salty sweat that had begun to form. He needed to run, now. Getting involved in politics and war was unconscionable. *And what if the Fortification rebels show up here? On my doorstep!* He paced the length of the room like a caged beast, his breath growing heavy and ragged.

He rested a while and then paced the ceiling until the pressure in his ears became too much to bear. He wasn't fond of the vice-chancellor but did not wish to see him overthrown and the idea that Eron had been murdered by these rebels was absurd.

His calls to Denlor went unanswered and he could not rely on Nylthia. There was only one person whom he could call.

Chapter 11

Skelos sensed Osaphar's disgust, although it was clear from his expression.

Osaphar's lips twitched and his eyes narrowed as Skelos told him of his near-death expedition with Elise and Tabiatha. No matter which way he spun the story, he came across as a coward and cowardice was not the Citizen way.

'You've had no contact with her since?' said Osaphar.

Skelos had invited Osaphar into his home with some hesitation. He knew he would berate him for what he had done. The Citizen had always judged him. Every question asked was a test, every answer a fail.

Skelos shook his head. 'She hasn't attempted to make any, and I'm unable to contact her. The hologram has gone.'

He was not surprised that 'Orel' had vanished from his home. She had delivered her message, and he had refused to hear it.

Osaphar sat in one of the dining room chairs. His pale green eyes made the room feel cold. 'What's the matter with you? You should have stayed to learn more.'

'In case you hadn't noticed, I have my own problems. I'm under investigation, my wife's left me, and my niece has only just returned.'

'And you don't think you owe our former Ruling Chancellor allegiance? You don't wish to avenge his death?'

Skelos harrumphed. He couldn't pretend he didn't care. Eron had been more of a brother to him than

Aughen had in his youth. He acted as if the passing of time had diminished those feelings, but they had not. He tried not to think about his childhood and the red dust from the caves. It was near impossible. As a child he had formed a strong bond — a brotherhood — with Osaphar and Eron that would never be broken or forgotten. Eron's wife and son had emigrated to a neighbouring planet away from the media glare and controversy that had followed his death.

He was determined to stand his ground. Regardless of his guilt, and the bond he had shared with Eron, he felt under no obligation to avenge his death. 'We were in danger. Elise wasn't thinking rationally. She intended to launch us into space in a primeval warship. I had to abort. And how could I trust her? She came out of nowhere. You have friends among the Parliamentary Elite, including my wife. You can take care of it, can you not? Osaphar, The Bold.'

Osaphar glared at him. 'Do *not* call me that,' he said. 'How are we to know our enemies from our foes?'

'I've no idea. Talk it through with Nythlia. I'm going to see my brother in Kaltharine and I'm taking Amelia with me. I'll send you a crate of Zaskian or two while I'm there.' He stood up and waited for Osaphar to do the same. He wanted to see him walk out of his front door. He did not want him loitering around the house, tormenting him as Orel had done short hours ago. He suspected he would regret revisiting the hydro-pod for the rest of his life.

Osaphar slammed his hand on the seat of his chair. 'Sit down!'

Skelos walked to the door. *Very well. If he shan't leave...* 'I have to pack.'

'Sit down, or I'll swear you'll regret it. You cannot deliver this information and walk away. This is beyond the two of us. You know this. You want to act like a Citizen.'

Skelos returned to face Osaphar. 'Of course, it's beyond the two of us,' he spat. 'That's what I've been trying to tell you. The Establishment believe I'm plotting against them. The incident in the sky today will only support their deluded beliefs. And you're right when you said we don't know our enemies from our foes. Someone has set me up to take the fall for this, and I'm not about to wait around here to let them do it.'

'They will catch up with you wherever you go.'

Skelos flopped into a chair. His heart raced in his chest. He could feel the dampness spreading across his forehead and down his back. How could he redeem himself if he ran from the very Citizens from whom he wanted approval?

'Is it possible you sent the signal without knowing it?' said Osaphar.

'I don't think so. I found the remote device in the glasshouse. I sat in the hydro-pod chair, but I'd done that before when I was a boy and no signal ever went out — that I know of.' He thought back over the last few days. 'I didn't do anything new. Nothing I hadn't done before.'

Osaphar raised an eyebrow. Skelos found himself blushing. He knew what Osaphar must have thought. He had never touched her in that way, but saying it wasn't going to make his former friend believe him. He had bought Orel out after Nythlia had left. Osaphar would naturally assume that it was to fulfil some kind of depraved need, no matter what he told him.

'Did you tell anyone else about the part-humanoid?'

'Denlor, but he didn't hear the message and I-I trust him with...' He trailed off. *How can I trust anyone, after all I have witnessed in the last forty-eight hours? I don't even trust myself.*

Osaphar nodded, accepting Skelos's word on the matter. 'If only there was a way to destroy the threat and the list, then Index Eleven would be thrown into disarray.' He gave him a measured look. 'The revolutionists wouldn't know who to trust. Each planet would be forced to act alone, which would increase the chance of them being brought to justice. That's if they're brave enough to attempt to execute their own rulers without intergalactic support. If Onas were solely responsible for Eron's death, the Establishment would have found some mitigating evidence, I'm certain.'

Eron had suffered a single shot to the head. It killed him instantly; his cells were not able to regenerate in time. The Establishment assumed that he was assassinated by another within the Parliamentary Elite because there was no evidence to the contrary. No one else had been shot, and the Establishment could find no one who had a personal vendetta against him. Eron's murderer was still out there, most likely on another planet.

It may have been too late to eliminate the threat. The signal had been sent. The wheels had been set in motion. But he could use his Gift to destroy the list – or expose it. That much he could do. *That and perhaps a little more...* 'I have a plan,' he said. It was as if the words were not his own. This was the Maker's Will; something that could not be explained.

'Please don't say murder because that would be—'

'No, not murder. Something a little less radical.'

After Osaphar had left, Skelos sent Zatar a message on the encrypted gateway and waited.

Chapter 12

Skelos slid the Datas card Osaphar had retrieved from the Thruen across the table to Zatar. He had arranged to meet him in the restaurant of a secluded town, one hundred miles from the city.

Zatar had been enjoying a large seafood platter when Skelos found him in the quiet restaurant. He licked his lips, savouring the flavours. He had been suspicious the moment Skelos had contacted him.

He took the Datas card, stared at it for a moment, and then passed it back to him. 'This means nothing to me. Who are you? What do you want?'

'Skelos.' He had no plans to divulge his surname. *Why risk unnecessary complications?* 'I was the one who sent the signal.'

Zatar nodded. He wiped his mouth on a napkin and took a gulp of wine. 'Elise told me about you. She said you denied sending the signal, and then jumped ship – literally.'

Skelos smiled. 'It was merely a test. You can never be too careful.'

'Your test could have cost me and my Denizen squad our lives if I had acted immediately, which I did not.'

Skelos felt his throat go dry. He poured himself a glass of water from the jug on the table. 'Because of what I told Elise?'

Zatar pushed his plate away. His appetite gone. 'No – because she was attacked by an unidentified ship.' He wagged his fork. 'You're not a member of the Parliamentary Elite, so why show me the card?'

'Someone tried to kill me. I found the Datas card on them. Now can you understand my caution? The assassination of President Tusan cannot go ahead. Not while we have a traitor in our midst.'

'And you think that has something to do with me?'

'How would I know? Would you tell me if it did?'

Zatar merely shrugged and signalled the waiter for more wine.

Skelos didn't know who might be watching or listening. The sooner he found that list, the sooner he could destroy it. 'I need to see the list. Where can I find it?'

Zatar drummed his hands together. 'Closer than you think.' He leaned forward, meeting Skelos's curious gaze. 'Though, it won't tell you who tried to kill you, if that's what you're thinking. There is only one Index Eleven file. It holds the list of every member. One member holds the list for four years and then passes it on to a successor. Names can be added on recommendation and removed upon request by any Index Eleven member.'

Skelos leaned away from him. 'So who has the list now?'

'Onas Pralyeton.'

At first his mother denied knowing anything about Index Eleven, but as he revealed what he knew of her involvement, the details came spilling out and it was more than he had suspected.

'I had nothing to do with Eron's death,' she said, her eyes downcast. 'I only joined the list to challenge the rule prohibiting the expansion of Dorm Presteria

Energy. The former Ruling Chancellor had blocked our efforts for too long. I wanted to provide more opportunities for our family. The list helped me achieve my goal. The rewards were instantaneous. It gave me the influence I needed to overcome the obstacles in my way. I had the hologram projector installed within the walls of our home to preserve it for the time we are called upon to do our part.'

It explained her reaction when he had asked her about the hydro-pod. He didn't want to argue further. All he wanted was the list. If its contents were revealed, it would condemn them all to far greater ruin than his failed demonstration ever could.

'The time is now,' said Skelos. 'You went to my vault. You took a file from it containing the list. Where is it?'

'I-I destroyed it. You needn't wor-worry any further.' Her bottom lip trembled as she struggled to get the words out. A tremor went through her body. She wrapped her arms around herself to quell it.

He studied her, taking in the gaunt lines on her face, her sorrowful expression. 'Spare me your lies. You and I both know it's not the original list.'

'What are you going to do?' She understood his Gift as a talent, something he had mastered to infiltrate technological systems. She had no idea it was some phenomena beyond even his control or understanding. It was the Maker's Will. 'There's a traitor in Index Eleven. They are going to ruin us.'

She shook her head fiercely. 'Don't do this, Skelos. You could put our lives in danger. I will never be able to return to Odisiris.'

'If the list is destroyed, there is no evidence to link you to it. You should be grateful. I'm doing us a service.'

'You are doing *me* a disservice. You don't know how hard I've worked to build our reputation and our legacy. Now you want to tear it down. You who have ruined us in the field of cybernetics. There are Citizens who block our access to the top, and there are ones who are willing to accommodate us. We cannot be seen to go against them. We need others to do that for us. This was why Index Eleven was created. Don't you dare do what I think you're going to do!'

'Having the House of Brailey name on Index Eleven could have been the end of us. And we don't need any more scandal hanging over our heads than we have already, do we, mother?'

Chapter 13

Skelos walked in on Nythlia and Onas embracing, their bodies pressed against each other, their lips locked. Skelos didn't think he had ever known Nylthia to kiss so passionately. The image stung him. But there was a greater betrayal. He waited for his blood to simmer before he passed the door's threshold.

He had never meant to be so bold. Onas was foolish enough to have cyborgs posted outside the door of his home. Cyborgs that he created and knew how to shut down even without his Gift.

In hindsight, he should have known there was someone else in Nylthia's life. She had been unwilling to give him a second chance after one catastrophic experiment.

On hearing his footsteps, the couple jolted to attention. Nylthia wiped her lips and turned away and Onas turned an unsightly shade of blue. An angry gleam came to his eyes when he saw it was Skelos who had disturbed him.

Nylthia attempted to compose herself. She smoothed down her hair, though there wasn't a strand out of place. 'Skelos, what are you doing here?'

'I came to see Onas,' he said, his eyes on the vice-chancellor's advisor. 'If you don't mind Nylthia, I wish to speak to Onas alone.'

'Wait for me in the dining room, Nylthia,' said Onas.

Blue blood crept up Nylthia's neck. She shared a final look with Onas and then left the room, trotting the last few steps to the door. It closed after her.

Onas proceeded to his desk, rubbing sweat from his hands and dabbing his forehead. 'Dr Skelos, I don't know what to say. I'm deeply ashamed, but Nythlia assured me that the marriage was to be terminated within the month. And I could not wait.' He drew himself up, raised his chin, and said with taunting arrogance, '*We* could not wait.'

Skelos tried to control his anger, to keep his blue blood creeping to the surface of his skin. 'Don't bother to explain yourself. I'm here on an entirely different matter. A deeply private one.'

Onas took a breath and lowered himself onto his desk chair. 'Talk freely. We are alone.'

Skelos knew this wasn't the case. That was the thing about being an Odisirian Citizen, you were never truly alone. Someone or something was always watching, tracking your every move. Thank the Maker, such technology did not hinder him. 'I want my Stores back and the go ahead to continue my research without interference.'

'Because of Nylthia. You threaten me with her?'

He threw the Datas card on the desk. 'I believe this belongs to you.'

Onas watched the card skim across the desk. He leaned back in his chair, his eyes bulging. 'That's not mine.'

'I know you wanted Osaphar and I dead. Somehow you found out we had a copy of Index Eleven and didn't want to risk exposure. You were ready to overthrow vice-chancellor, Gabe Nevassi and wanted to leave nothing to chance. You were never interested in my particular field of research, were you? I know you used your son to spy on me. You saw me as a threat. All because of the list. It may interest you to know that

I too have joined the Index. If I'm honest, I'm insulted you left me off it in the first place.'

Onas cleared his throat. 'You can't have joined. I would have been informed.'

'Because you have the original list?' He nodded. 'Yes, Zatar told me. You can verify it for yourself.'

'Have you told Nythlia of this?'

Onas's question confirmed Nythlia knew nothing about Index Eleven. It gave him some small relief. 'I don't trust her, but I trust you. We have the same ambition, the same drive, and the same amount to lose.' The remark was flippant. He had no inkling of what Onas held most dear or the risks he was willing to take to assume power.

Onas waved his hand. 'Take off your clothes.'

'Excuse me?' *This is a risk too far, even for me!*

'Somehow you managed to get past my sentinel guards. I need to see you have no devices or weapons on you.' He directed Skelos to a changing screen. A sentinel guard stood beside it.

Skelos went behind the screen and removed his outer garments. He soon emerged from behind it dressed only in his underwear.

He winced as the sentinel guard patted him down with its cold metallic hands.

'He is clean,' said the sentinel in a resonance of an echo.

It returned to its place by the changing screen.

Onas removed a disk from a flap on his wrist device. He twisted the disk to unlock it. Then, with a subtle hum, a grid of light emerged an inch above the disk. It grew outward, taking the form of a hologram screen sprung from it. He scanned its contents. Three organised columns of names stood out against the transparent backdrop. Onas found Skelos's name midway down the list, beside his mother's.

'You were once a close friend of Eron's. It's the sole reason you were not considered. Some thought you might attempt to avenge his death.' He snorted. 'I was sceptical about that myself. I don't think former friends count, do you? What was it you fell out over? A girl, finance, business?'

'He didn't support my work–my research.' Skelos was too young to have conducted any research and the admission made no sense whatsoever to a Citizen like Onas. He and Eron had fallen out because of what Skelos had done in the Red Caves as a child. Skelos had kept both Osaphar and Eron at a distance after that and they had done the same. Following the event, he was ashamed of what he had done in his childish naivety. He later came to justify his actions. It was not an atrocity if the child was an Outsider. Despite the humanoid form they took, they were diseased beasts.

'I want to show you what we've done to some of your cyborgs.'

Skelos glanced up as a faint whoosh sounded from across the large room. A rectangular section of the wall slid into the floor, revealing an entrance. Two armour-clad figures emerged, walking in unison: one male; one female. Their limbs moved with mechanical precision. Their faces were flawless recreations of synthetic skin – too flawless to be humanoid.

'We've built in more weaponry. These ones are prototypes. They will eventually become droids that will look and move like humanoids.'

Skelos scoffed, unimpressed and unconvinced. He had never come across a droid who could past for human. 'Who's we?'

'I'm in the process of opening up my own cybernetic research facility.'

Now it made sense. 'In my former Stores, I presume.' He suspected Nythlia was behind Onas's cybernetic ascendency. The Citizen held no doctorate. He guessed he had not only secured his Stores but his staff as well. He wondered if Denlor was on his payroll. Onas would have also asked his son, Imbrecas, to steal vital information about his work so he could replicate it. *With his limited attention span, the boy couldn't possibly have succeeded.* 'And the Establishment have approved it?'

'Not yet, but they will.' He gave the cyborgs an appraising glance. 'This pair will never be seen by the Establishment. They are our Index Eleven assassin cyborgs, and they answer to my command alone.' He gave a sly grin.

Skelos focused on the hologram. He closed his eyes and raised his hands momentarily to force his Gift to the forefront of his mind and put it to work. Data-streams from the surrounding systems flowed through his mind's eye.

The names on the list disappeared one by one as he forwarded them to the Parliamentary suite where the vice-chancellor, Darlis Sajoyagh, was meeting with several other prominent members of the Establishment.

Onas's mouth fell open. He stared through the hologram and met Skelos's eyes. He grabbed the disk from the table, moving the screen. He tried to close the disk shut. With shaking hands, he twisted it clockwise and counter-clockwise. He banged it on the desk. The names kept vanishing. 'You!' he bellowed. He lurched from his chair. 'How are you making this happen?'

'It has nothing to do with me.' Skelos raised his hands. Only two names remained — his mother's and his own. 'It must be a virus.'

While Onas continued to obsess over the missing files, Skelos sprang into action. With practiced precision, both physical and mental, he directed the female cyborg into position. Before Onas could look up from his workstation, the cyborg swung into motion. Its steel limbs detached Onas's head from his neck in a swift, slicing movement. A shrill alarm sounded from the security hub, followed by another that sputtered like a dying engine.

Skelos wasted no time, signalling to the cyborgs with his mind to destroy any evidence. As the cyborgs set to dismantling the surveillance systems, he gathered his belongings with haste. Just as he swept from the room, the sound of pursuing Citizens echoed down the corridor. Weaving through the facility, he slipped past two sentinel guards posted at the exit. Their photoreceptor eyes scanned him without recognition or concern.

None who saw him that day would confirm his presence. The only witness to his actions was Nylthia, and they both knew if she spoke up, she would go down with him. The only living witness who could identify him was Nelly, and if she sought to bring him down, she would only succeed in destroying herself along with him.

Chapter 14

Skelos took in the lavish decor as he sat in the Gold Suite. Gold coated every surface as far as the eye could see—the walls, the floor, the ornate trim around each doorway. He ran his fingers along the plush material of the couch, feeling its soft texture. This room had always been Nylthia's domain for entertaining the rare political dignitaries who visited their estate. He had never been present for those gatherings. *I can't recall the last time I stepped foot in here.* A decade ago, perhaps, for some occasion he no longer remembered. And Nythlia had made it clear through her icy demeanour that his presence was unwanted.

He sipped from a flute brimming with Zaskian. It warmed his throat as it went down. The events of the past three weeks had drained him. The sacrifices he had made were taking their toll. Several prominent shareholders had pulled out of Dorm Presteria Energy, figures who had helped raise the company and industry to acclaim. But now they felt the House of Dorm was fading, more an embarrassment than a source of influence.

His mother was so angered over the list's dissolution; she had cut all ties with him. He had grown fed up with his mother's griping and felt no remorse for what he had done. She should have been nothing but grateful in his opinion. He had saved them from a fate worse than death. She didn't seem to grasp the peril they had narrowly avoided from having been on the list in the first place.

He began to care less about the family name and more about his own. *Surely that's all that matters now?* His hopes of making recompense were crippled. He had gained a reputation as an unethical scientist. As a result, his fellow Citizens were less keen to open their research facilities to him. Denlor was the only one of his staff to remain in contact. His last faithful confidante.

The destruction of the list had caused a brief ripple among the Establishment. Some of its members had resigned; others had mysteriously vanished. Vacant posts were quickly filled without scandal or skirmish.

Onas's death was believed to be caused by a batch of malfunctioning cyborgs, which Nythlia had corroborated. Skelos knew she wanted to remove herself from any scandal linked to Index Eleven, and thus to Onas. It was the only way she could protect her career.

Denlor had informed him that Nythlia had not attended Onas's funeral, but he had seen her walking with Imbrecas, a protective arm around his shoulder. No doubt offering him comfort following the tragic death of his father.

A cyborg showed Osaphar through to the Gold Suite. Skelos had been expecting him. Though they were once close friends, a sense of unease had come over him in the lead up to this meeting. He did not know how much Osaphar knew of his current role or the contents of Index Eleven. Most of all, he feared being questioned on whether he had destroyed it as promised long ago, or if those dangerous secrets still existed somewhere in the Vega's vast digital network. He hoped he wouldn't ask.

'I don't know how you were able to do it,' said Osaphar as he breezed through the door, 'but thank the Maker you did. I assume Onas was involved. I take it you were responsible for his death?'

'In self-defence,' said Skelos, not bothering to deny it. 'He possessed the original list. He was going to turn one of his cyborg assassins on me.'

'You should have left it to the Establishment to punish him.'

'Is that all you can say, after all I have accomplished?' *You're no more grateful than my mother.* 'He was building cyborg assassins. He slept with my wife.'

Osaphar was silent for a time. 'So you killed him out of jealousy,' he finally said.

Skelos bristled. 'Stop pretending you're Eron. You're nothing like him. You act like you have morals. You would have done the same. Do not speak of my past demeanours ever again. I cannot rewrite history. I've lost my family to avenge Eron's death. You were the one who coaxed me into it. And what have I gained?' He spread his hands. 'The right to sit in the Gold Suite.'

'You're right, I'm not Eron. But don't try to hold me responsible for what *you* have done. I don't think with your particular *talents* it would have been too hard to get your hands on that list or to destroy it.'

'What's that supposed to mean?'

Osaphar took a ragged breath. His words were laboured as he spoke. 'That I commend you. I assume you don't have a backup plan.'

'None. Now will you stay and have a drink?'

'No. I think we're done here. I thank you for your assistance.' Osaphar walked from the suite with hurried steps.

It seems he does did not want to renew our friendship after all.

Skelos smashed his glass of Zaskian against the gold-tiled floor in frustration. Alcohol and glass shards flew everywhere. He stormed out of the suite, vowing to have the entire space redecorated in blue by the end of the week.

He took the lift down to the basement. He had converted the open space into a makeshift laboratory. It wasn't the most suitable location for his experiments but it would have to do for now. He hoped one day to find a permanent facility.

His latest specimen lay unconscious on a metal table. It was time to create something new, he thought — a cybernetically enhanced human to rival even Orel. One who would be loyal and obedient, whom he could trust without reservation, and who would never abandon him. *And why not?* "You should never place your full trust in any single individual", his father had taught him before disappearing from his life.

He didn't want to make another Tabiatha. She was too extreme. He wanted something subtler yet dependable. And there would be no prototypes or room for error. Only success.

With a steady hand and some strategic modifications, I think I can improve upon the original design. He took a deep breath to steady his nerves, picked up a scalpel, and made the first incision into Amelia's brain.

Part 2

The
Red Caves

Chapter 15

Six years have passed since Skelos's first experiments, all tried and tested, failed before the Pareus Scientific Research and Funding Division (P.S.R.F.), in a demonstration that left his subject brain dead. The P.S.R.F. has withdrawn his funding. The Planetary Protection Committee has confiscated the majority of his research, the Parliamentary Elite has frozen his assets, and he has lost his credibility as a scientist.

The Red Caves was the last place on the planet of Odisiris where the Establishment would find him. The caves no longer held the allure of mystery that had attracted him in his youth. The young Citizens[2] of the modern age were not interested in Outsiders. Their veil of mystery was broken when one was captured and brought to the city of Pareus and paraded in a cage for all of Odisiris to see. The ill-fated Outsider had carried a pox-like disease. Now this race of sub-humans was seen as a scourge that required extermination. It had taken place to some extent. The Odisirian government had sent a team of Eradicators to the Red Caves. They had released a poison into the tunnels to kill all living things that dwelt there, and they had erected an electromagnet barrier to keep them from escaping. Still some survived. The caves and tunnels went deep. There were many exits and entrances the Citizens knew nothing about.

---

[2] <u>Citizens</u> – race of superhumans from the planet Odisiris, located within the Andromeda Galaxy.

The barrier was not a deterrent for Dr Skelos Dorm. He knew how to disable it and once he had brought it down, he waited. Waited for the fear to ebb away. He let the red dust settle on his skin. He gasped and shuddered. He sucked air through his nostrils and shuddered again. There was nothing to fear. *I'm all alone. My race has abandoned me.*

'Are we here now?' said Amelia.

Okay, so he wasn't entirely alone. He had his niece. The little girl accompanied him everywhere. He took her hand. He did not want her to see his fear. She would not understand it.

She was covered from head to foot in the red grime. He had heard a myth that Outsiders blood made the dust red. He knew this not to be true. But the dust repulsed him all the same. It reminded him of another little girl. 'We most certainly are.'

They went through the squat cave entrance. Skelos had not forgotten it. The structure had not changed, nor had his memory of it. He had not forgotten the little girl he had killed as a child. The girl was not much older than Amelia. He could still see her red dust-caked tears, the hole he had blasted in her shoulder, and the red blood.

A minute flare drone led the way, drifting through the succession of tunnels that connected the caves. Skelos hoped the child's remains were buried under a pile of rock and dust. His heart pounded. He steamed along, gazing ahead, afraid the memories would fester in his brain if he were to stop. The tunnel was more cramped now that he was taller and a lot larger around the waist. The fear and exhilaration he felt in equal measure, when he had entered the Red Caves more than thirty years ago were no longer there.

This was a necessity. A desperate necessity.

'You're walking too fast, Uncle,' said the little girl, skipping to keep up with him.

'It's not that I am walking too fast,' he said, picking up his pace, 'it is *you* who are walking too slowly.'

'We shouldn't have to walk at all,' she said, trying to tug her hand free from his.

Skelos ignored her. The girl was spoilt. Spoilt to the core. His brother and sister-in-law had given her everything she had ever wanted, and he had picked up where they left off.

After walking a considerable distance, with Amelia whinging in his ear, Skelos discovered the cave suited his needs.

A layer of red dust coated the bronze walls. Piles of debris littered the ground, cracked in places to reveal another makeshift shelter below. The size and temperature of the cave felt just right - not too extreme in either direction. Indentations and nooks along the cave walls provided plenty of spots to store his utensils.

As he explored the far end of the cave, he discovered an anti-chamber filled with junk and debris. At first, he assumed it was items stolen from the Citizens by the Outsiders. However, after a quick look around, he realised that wasn't the case. Some of the objects were unlike anything he had seen before—ancient, man-made, foul-smelling and covered in mould. There was no need to clean it out since the main area of the cave was spacious enough.

The mouldy odour he could tolerate. But the dust was too much. It was everywhere. In his mind, he saw himself breathing it in and then spewing red blood.

Amelia squirmed. She shook the skirt of her dress. 'I don't like it, Uncle. It's dirty.'

'Yes, very.'

'But who's going to clean it, Uncle? We don't have any droids.'

'We're going to clean it.'

Amelia's mouth formed an O-shape. 'We?'

'Yes, *we*. We might as well get it out of the way since we're here. It shan't take long. You will use rags and water to get some of the dust off these walls, and you can use this,' he kicked at a rudimentary tool: a wooden pole with a brush attached to the end of it, 'on the floors. I will clear the rubble by hand.'

The little girl pouted. 'But my dress will get ruined.'

'Most likely, but you've plenty more dresses.'

'This is my best one. I'm not a cleaner. Mummy said I'm too pretty and delicate for manual labour. And this is a cave, isn't it supposed to be dirty?'

Skelos held up his hand to silence her. 'If I say you'll clean, you'll clean. If you want to act as my assistant then you will, at times, be required to do jobs below your status. Do you understand?'

The little girl bowed her head. 'Yes, Uncle.'

By the time Amelia had finished, her dress was filthy and torn. Despite her grumbling, she had done a good job.

Skelos had pushed most of the rubble out of the cave and into the adjoining tunnels.

Exhausted, they returned to Pareus city.

He was satisfied he could continue his work without the Establishment on his back, or any of the others who conspired against him and had relished in his downfall. And he knew there were many.

He slept peacefully that night. His newly acquired specimen, lay in her own bed, three doors away in a drug induced sleep. Amelia slept in her cot in the far corner of the room where he could keep an eye on her.

Chapter 16

The following morning, they rose with the sun and took a short flight back to the caves on a small glider.

Skelos lifted his heavily sedated subject out of the vehicle. He hoisted the woman over his shoulder. She hardly weighed anything. Still, handling her caused him some discomfort. Her jutting bones struck his sides. Her hair scratched his face. Her skin had a crepe-like texture that reminded him of the skin of a dead lizard.

He had the good sense to wear a face mask. He didn't feel the dust in his throat. The fear that had almost consumed him the day before had subsided.

To pacify Amelia, he had brought a house droid with him. He had also brought the few crates of equipment he had managed to salvage from his old Stores[3]. The droid carried the crates on the steel forks fitted to the base of its shell.

Once in the new laboratory, the droid unpacked the crates.

Skelos lowered his sedated subject onto the floor. He propped her against a wall and wrapped a folded blanket around her neck to prevent it flopping about. The last thing he wanted was for her neck to snap. Good specimens were hard to come by.

Amelia sat obediently in her chair, awaiting her instructions. She wore a blue silk dress with a voluminous skirt and had insisted on bringing two more with her, in case another got ruined on account of his 'cleaning demands'.

---

[3] <u>Stores</u> – research facility.

He detested the dresses and the ribbons as much as his ex-wife, Nylthia. But he had never denied her a dress or a ribbon. He owed her that much.

He dragged a hologram chart from his tablet of notes. He heard a faint sound, so faint that he supposed he could have ignored it. Ordinarily, he would have. However, it reminded him that he hadn't gone to the trouble of checking the adjoining vicinities. He had ceased his exploration of the caves when he had found the space he was looking for. Perhaps he had been too confident no one else was around. *I should check. Just to be sure.*

'Wait here,' he told Amelia.

'Why, Uncle? Where are you going?'

The girl asked too many questions for his liking. 'To look around. You keep a close eye on our subject.'

Her eyes widened. 'But what if she wakes? What shall I do?'

Bash her over the head with my tablet. 'Scream.'

The little girl nodded, happy with his response.

Chapter 17

Skelos brought the house droid along as an emergency plan. Its metal frame would draw attention if needed. He hurried through the first tunnel; feet unsteady in the dim light.

The path split again and again before him. Some passages glowed with luminous stone outlining their walls. Others appeared untouched for centuries based on the thick dust coating the ground. A few tunnels seemed packed tight by mud. The smell of death lingered heavily in some tunnels, and the wind's howl echoed down others.

As he pressed on, he kept a close eye on his route tracker. The device would ensure he found his way back. He had no intention of getting lost. Not this time.

He eventually found the source of the faint sound. It belonged to one of them: the scourge. The diseased cattle.

The Outsider stood in a cave bigger than the one Skelos had discovered and made his own. He realised he should have made the effort to venture further in search of a laboratory. This one would have better suited his needs. Its shelves were hewn from clefts. It had tables created from stacked rock slabs, all burdened with mysterious objects.

He thought of the inexplicable pile of junk in his ante-chamber. It had never occurred to him that Outsiders had their own belongings. No doubt, they had stolen them from someone, somewhere.

The Outsider's hair was matted and thick with white dust. His face was scrawny and lined. He wore a cotton shirt with the sleeves pushed up. A pair of odd looking transparent goggles covered his eyes. He stood next to a metal table with wheels and a box-shaped monitor with a cracked screen. Skelos noted other pieces of machinery with wires attached to them. He saw mechanical keyboards and other apparatus he did not recognise.

'You looking for something,' said the Outsider.

He had a crisp accent, one Skelos couldn't place. It was not surprising. He had never heard one speak. But he had heard them scream. *He doesn't carry himself like an Outsider.* He was not hunched over or rattling with fear. He stood straight and proud. His eyes were alive with...*indignation.* His clothes, which had once been pristine, were soiled rags.

'Doctor Oliver Best.' He approached Skelos with his right hand outstretched.

It has no Mark! 'Don't you dare touch me,' he snapped.

Outsiders did not have professions, or so he was made to understand by the Establishment. Outsiders couldn't hold conversations. They were an insipid breed who could barely walk upright. You hardly needed a profession to scurry after lizards in the dirt. But some of the utensils the Outsider possessed appeared to be crude twisted versions of his own.

Not an Outsider, Skelos concluded, *but an Unmarked One all the same.* He had to presume he was a stowaway who came from another planet.

'You seem a little skittish. Are you new?'

'How dare you question me. How long have you been here?'

'About a year.' The Outsider looked him up and down. 'You're from out there, aren't you?' He sighed and bowed his head. 'Who sent you?'

'No one sent me.' Skelos continued to gaze around the cave. There were so many things, so many things he had never seen before. Where had they all come from?

'But you are a Citizen. You're not tolerant of any other race.'

'Not true, and it has nothing to do with tolerance.' Tolerance was too gracious a word for Pareusians's to associate with Outsiders. 'How did you end up here? Where did you come from?'

'I would likely tell you if I thought you would believe me, and I trusted you. I don't know you well enough to trust you. Suffice to say, I was not born in the Red Caves. I merely seek refuge here.'

'A clever answer.' And one Skelos felt comfortable with for the moment. 'What are you a doctor of?'

'Medicine,' replied Oliver.

How dull. 'I'm a doctor also.'

'Your field?'

'Neuroscience.' *Should I have told him that?* He gestured to the cave. 'What is all this equipment?'

'Old technology. Instruments from the past. I found most of it. I imagine it's been here for years.'

Skelos nodded to a half-rusting metal table on wheels. He pictured Ishara Molari on it. It would take her weight. 'And this is where you sleep?'

'No. I sleep on the ground.' Oliver placed his hand on the wheeled table. This is a gurney.'

Skelos gave him an inquisitive look. 'For patients?'

Specimens.

The corners of Oliver's mouth turned upward in a smile, revealing teeth stained by years of neglect. 'You're either a visionary – or you've seen one of these before.'

No life-chambers or beds. 'Then I'm a visionary.'

He stared around again. Dr Best stepped aside to allow him to do so.

His gaze settled on a rack of trays laden with needles and plungers.

'Syringes,' said Oliver. 'You slot needles into them and administer the drug to your patient or use it to withdraw blood.'

Skelos had figured this out for himself, simply by the shape of the instrument. Dr Best pointed out more things to him: electrode gel pads, an ECG machine, amethyst drug jars, a machine that required a turnstile to play music, a steam kettle, a Culpeper microscope, a heart monitor... the list went on.

Oliver informed him on a manner of instruments and equipment and how they worked. Skelos forgot that he was conversing with an Unmarked One.

He found the Doctor of Medicine to be articulate and intelligent.

By the time Oliver had finished giving him a tour of the cave, he was standing alongside him, squeezing some electrode gel on the back of his hand.

'Is there anything here you like?' said Oliver.

Skelos had seen many instruments he could make use of. 'Are you offering them?'

Oliver chuckled. 'In return for payment.'

'Payment?'

'What can you do with payment?' Skelos liked him less now he had the gall to ask to be paid for archaic equipment, most of which had never belonged to him in the first place. And payment requests were the rights of Citizens – no one else.

'Go to Brevons Beach.'

Brevons Beach was the home to mercenaries and gamblers. It was not a place for Citizens. Not First Status Citizens or Second, *perhaps not even Third.*

'You seriously think I need these things?'

'I do. You don't strike me as a collector of antiques. You need these things, and you're desperate. Desperate to conceal your business in this wasteland. You're desperate to stay, and I'm desperate to leave. I can tell you how to work the equipment.'

Skelos produced a thin metal card from his pocket. It held six hundred nano-credits, though the amount was not printed upon it. He had a few others tucked away holding even larger stores of credit, enough to get him past any planetary authorities without a trace. Without a way to scan the credits himself, the doctor took the card with a nod of thanks.

'I'll want these things boxed up.'

Oliver nodded. 'I'll draw up a list. You can come here any time and get more, if others haven't gotten to it by then. Let's make a start. I want to leave tonight.'

Chapter 18

With his new laboratory complete, Skelos set about testing his ECG machine. It worked as the doctor said it would.

Dr Oliver Best had also given him an electricity generator. But Skelos didn't need it.

He used his Gift to bring the ECG machine to life. It beeped. The display panel came on.

'Where did you get all this junk from, Uncle?' said Amelia as she cleaned the gurney. She wore a pair of his surgical gloves not meant for her tiny hands; she struggled to hold her cleaning cloth because the fingers dangled well past her wrists.

He insisted she do a thorough job of cleaning the rust-infested gurney. Who knew who had handled the instruments before him? He didn't want to catch anything.

'I bought them from a merchant.'

Amelia stayed quiet for a full ten minutes, mulling this over. 'But it's old,' she said eventually. 'Why would you buy old things?' She leaned into her work, intent on removing every speck of dirt or grime from the metal surface. She had polished it so much it gleamed.

Skelos discovered the house droid broken in the corner. As he walked over for a closer look, he saw its metal plating had been smashed inward. Kneeling down, he picked up a piece of the casing—two deep impressions, from a petite boot print, were stamped into the metal. Acid had been poured over its circuits. Someone hadn't just damaged the droid, they had deliberately destroyed it. 'What happened to the droid?'

'I don't know. Its circuits got all burned up. I don't think it could cope with all the dust.'

Another noise disturbed him. Voices. Faint and unfamiliar. No footsteps.

He left Amelia to her cleaning.

He took to the myriad of tunnels, racing along in a torrent of fear. His Bolt-Shot Whip in one hand, a laser gun in the other. He walked for longer than he had done the last time. The voices took him in a new direction, far from Dr Oliver Best's chamber of treasures, far from his own. The voices confused him. They rose and died, rose and died, and they changed direction. They bounced off the walls, now distant to his left, now close above.

At last he found them concealed behind a bulging wall of rock.

He was hesitant. He didn't think it was possible to be caught so soon, but he couldn't be sure. It would not bode well for him if there were other Citizens in the Caves. Not when he had made so much progress in so short a time.

Two men were in conversation. One had a strong dominant voice, the other spoke in low whispery tones. *One of them cares not to be heard, the other can't care less.*

He was as close as he could get. He stood on the other side of the back of a cave. He found a small crevice belching air. He pressed his body flat against the warm stone and peered through the narrow opening.

He saw the back of one of the men, his face obscured by a bone-white hood. He could hardly see

crystal orbs. But surely it wasn't Zichronite that caused the Shards to melt. Perhaps the globe was hot. But then if it were hot, why would the Hooded Man continue to cup it with his bare hands?

'It's beautiful,' said the Greasy-Haired One.

'Is it?' asked the Hooded Man.

The colours penetrated the walls. Skelos was thinking about how close they were to his new laboratory and about what the two men would do if they were to discover it. He had to make sure that didn't happen.

The Greasy-Haired One stood stiff and motionless, eyes fixed on the globe. Blood trickled from his nose onto his lip. The man licked his tongue.

Skelos recoiled slightly. Red Blood caught in the glare of colours. It had been a long time since he had seen the blood of an Unmarked One.

'May I go?' said the Greasy-Haired One.

Skelos flattened himself against the rough wall and held his breath. *No, not yet.* He did not want the Greasy-Haired One to see him, and he got the impression the demonstration was not over.

'Not before you have taken your own life,' the Hooded Man said.

The bare-chested man's brows dipped in confusion. His nostrils flared. 'With what?'

Skelos wasn't certain he had heard right. Was that what he meant when he said, 'May I go?' It crossed his mind that he had stumbled upon some strange ritual. And the nature of the men's agreement was suicide.

'With the blade you hold behind your back,' said the Hooded Man, 'the one you were going to plunge into my neck as you watched me observe the Avu'lore; the artefact I am using to control you.'

The Greasy-Haired One smiled. 'My apologies.' He brought a large, serrated knife from behind his back and slit his own throat in one clean sweep. The blood bubbled from the wound. He fell to the ground and the knife with him.

The Hooded Man stood frozen, as still as the ancient walls surrounding him. Five minutes passed. Then, slowly, he withdrew his hands from the globe where the Shards reemerged. One by one he wrapped them back in the cloth. He did the same with the globe. He slipped the Shards and the globe inside. He slid the compartment shut. There was no sign that it had ever been there.

He then moved over to the body of the dead man, which was still oozing blood. He picked up the knife and placed it on the dead man's chest. He then pulled out a small object that resembled a bundle of metal fibres. He held it over the Greasy-Haired One's corpse. White glowing threads appeared over the body. When the glow subsided, all signs of the man's end had vanished as had the knife and the trailing blood.

Skelos suppressed a gasp. The Hooded Man had frozen – still — as if he were listening for something.

He dashed back to the laboratory. The Hooded Man was not a Citizen, and he was not of his world.

Chapter 19

Skelos returned to his new laboratory and spent an hour trying to conceal its entrance lest the Hooded Man found him. He could barely think straight. If he was going to find a new location, he would need a minimum of two days—more—if he wanted to clear up after himself and dump the elder Citizen. He couldn't just pack up and run.

But in the back of his mind, he didn't see the need to go anywhere. Always captivated by anything to do with the mind, he resolved to take the Avu'lore for himself. It would be an asset to his collection. He desired power. Knowledge was power. Wealth brought power to some degree; Odisiris was swamped in it. He needed an advantage. The Avu'lore had the potential to change his life. Of course, he needed to understand how it worked. He thought it might even help accelerate his research.

He spent the next three hours fussing over his instruments and scolding his niece for trying to make conversation with the elderly Citizen in the bottom of the pit he had created for her.

Once Amelia had drifted off to sleep and the old woman had stopped moaning with the help of the sedative he had given her, Skelos left his laboratory and went in search of the cave where he had seen the Avu'lore. He couldn't wait another day. He had to have it. The power had to be within the Avu'lore itself, not in the one who wielded it.

He had no reason to be afraid. He had Citizen blood running through his veins; he needed to remember that. Since his fateful demonstration, he often second-guessed himself. He had managed to maintain the arrogance of his race. His confidence, however, came in waves of bold certainty, delusion, and doubt.

He didn't have voices to help him track down his prize, he had his memories and the scant markings he had made on the tunnel walls on his way back.

As a child he became lost in the caves and had spent hours in tears trying to find his way out. He had the fortitude to guarantee it didn't happen again. There would be no frantic blubbing and panic. Not this time.

He knew the gamble he was taking, leaving his laboratory unguarded twice, so soon after his arrival. He could bump into the Hooded Man and then what would become of him? *I shall kill him if he challenges me or anyone else who dares to stand in my way.*

He always felt that his tongue was his secret weapon and that if he kept it wagging long enough, something of value was bound to slip out. But the temptation of the Avu'lore was too great.

Portions of the wall wore a coat of green and orange fungi while the ground beneath was blanketed in what looked to be sand, despite the nearest shore lying a thousand miles distant.

He shone his night-light into the shaft's depths. Content that nothing was on its way up, he sprinted inside, sparing a quick glance over his shoulder. He stared at the pedestal where he had seen the demonstration and the spot where he had seen the Greasy-Haired One fall. There was no blood. No signs of life.

The Unmarked One had been teleported away. *But where?* And he had never seen a teleportation device mop up blood, not in his world, unless it was a new development he had not been made privy to. Such inventions would become known to the public once they had been fully tested. It was a good way to mop up, if you didn't have a droid, or a pole with a brush attached to one end of it. When he returned to Pareus he planned to make enquiries, and by make enquiries he meant ask his trusted confidant, the Third Status Citizen, Denlor.

He placed his hand on the section of the wall, retracing the movements of the Hooded Man. He waited. Had he touched the right place? Or had the Hooded Man used a device, some gadget, which caused the rock compartment to open?

He was starting to lose hope when his fingers paused over a spot that felt slightly smoother than the rest. *Can this be it?* He heard a faint scraping sound. A sliver of darkness appeared before him as the stone slab slid open, revealing its treasures.

He took out the two bundles: one containing the Avu'lore globe and the other the Shards. He felt inside the compartment to see if there was anything else of value. The globe was heavier than he expected, but his robes were filled with vast pockets and folds, big enough to hide the apparatus. He popped the globe and the Shards into the folds. He slid the rock drawer back into place and with one last look around the cave, he made his way back to his laboratory.

He returned to find his niece playing with a smoke-filled vial. He snatched it from her. 'How many times have I told you not to touch anything without my permission?'

She shrugged. 'Sorry, Uncle, you weren't here to ask.'

His eyes narrowed. Her insolence was a curse. Sometimes he could have sworn that she understood more than the House of Dorm had taught her, that there was great wisdom beneath the flatness in her eyes, her tranquil demeanour, and the layers of frills and silk. *There will be a place for her in the Parliamentary Elite if she keeps this up.*

'Help me with this.' He placed his newly acquired treasures on his work table.

Amelia clasped her hands together, smiling. 'Oh, what is it? Is it a present for me?'

'No, but it may help the both of us. You can unwrap it.'

Amelia unwrapped both bundles with the eagerness of any child accepting a gift. When she saw what lay inside, she stuck out her bottom lip and strutted back to her chair. 'I don't like it.'

'Because it's not a dress?' he asked.

'No, because it's boring.'

He used a metal tong to handle one of the Shards, gingerly lifting it at one end. He let it drop. On closer inspection he wasn't sure if they were made of glass; they felt like glass, but when the tongs hit them, they didn't make the chinking sound that glass made. He rubbed the Shards down with some alcohol, removed his gloves, Rolling the smooth, cool fragment between finger and thumb, its nature remained unclear. He put it to his ear and then slotted it under one of the antique microscopes he had acquired from Dr Oliver Best's hoard.

He could see the faint traces of Zichronite within it, grains of spectral colours. There was probably something else there too, something his eyes couldn't catch. It couldn't have been Zichronite alone that allowed the Hooded Man to control minds. It had to be something more. *How is it possible that an Unmarked One could make such a discovery where a Citizen of Odisiris could not?* Zichronite had a great many uses in Odisiris. It could be used to conduct energy, power turbines, generate heat, fuel airships; but to control the mind and turn a perfectly practical Citizen into a puppet – now that was debatable.

He slotted the Shards into the globe. As the colours began to appear, Amelia bounced over to him and leaned in, captivated by the pretty hues forming before her eyes.

He laid his hands on the globe's smooth surface. He didn't feel anything at all and thought he should have. The Hooded Man had exhibited a reverence of sorts when he had touched it. There was a sinking and rising of the chest, a momentum in the fingers. He tried to think how long the Hooded Man had waited before issuing a command. If he timed it correctly, it was less than a minute.

He tested his theory on his niece. 'Sit down, Amelia,' he said.

'No. I want to watch the pretty colours.'

Was the Avu'lore having the opposite effect? He shouldn't have needed the Avu'lore to get Amelia to do as he asked.

He attempted another command. 'Sit down on the floor.'

'But I don't want to. You said to sit on my chair.'

Perhaps, it's not the Avu'lore that's the problem. Perhaps it's Amelia. She was not just flesh, blood and bone. It was possible her robotic parts hindered the Avu'lore in some way.

He clicked his tongue and removed his hands from the globe, taking out the Shards. He tapped one of the Shard's on the table. Unless the Zichronite held it in place, this was no ordinary glass.

If he could penetrate the Shard, he could extract a particle. However, he lacked the proper tools to test the Shards or the globe, which meant he would have to return to the city and ask Denlor to help him obtain what he needed from his former Stores.

He had not given Denlor the location of his new laboratory, more out of embarrassment than trust. He would lose Denlor's respect if he revealed he had sunk to such an unimaginable low.

He considered returning to Oliver's hoard. He might find something there he could use. Then again, the risk was greater now he had the Avu'lore. He imagined the Hooded Man was scouring the tunnels and caves in search of his treasure.

Time was running out. With each passing moment, the secrets within the mysterious artifact seemed to slip further from his grasp.

Chapter 20

He mumbled to himself as he set about undoing the silver rope wrapped around the old woman's wrists and ankles. His hair was drenched with sweat from nerves and not with the burden of carrying her.

After spending the previous night cooped up and struggling at the back of the cave, the old woman lay quiet and exhausted.

Unable to listen to any more of her pitiful cries, he had not removed the tape from her mouth.

Ishara Molari was two hundred years old, although she could easily have passed for seventy. Her silver-grey hair swept her shoulders. Her eyes were shut tight as if they, too, were bound.

Supporting Ishara's full weight on his shoulders, he took her to the gurney. She hung around his neck like a flaccid scarf. But unlike a scarf, she was neither warm nor thick.

He had trained his night-light on the rusty gurney and the white flat screen in the centre of the cave. The Avu'lore, which would be central to his experiments, sat on a steel pedestal. It diverted attention from the surrounding clutter of outdated equipment and technology.

When Amelia saw him carrying the old woman, she remained seated against her better judgement. 'What are you going to do, Uncle?'

'Quiet. Help me.'

The child stood with some reluctance and watched him hoist Ishara onto the gurney.

The last two interlocking discs on Skelos's black laboratory coat popped open. His physique bore the weight of his labour. Literally. He had an extra twelve pounds of fat around his middle; the harder he worked the more he ate.

Ishara's bare feet acted with a will of their own, fighting stubbornly to stay on the ground. Her face was set with determination to use what little strength she had left for one final protest.

Once he had positioned her on the gurney, he gathered the straps that hung on either side of it. He fastened them around her small waist, feet, and shoulders, doubting he would need them at all once the drug had taken effect.

Amelia stood with her arms crossed, peering into the old woman's motionless face as if willing her eyes to open.

'Don't just stand there,' he said. 'Put some gel on those pads. We don't have all night.' *I have all day and all night. This is what I do. This is my life.*

His work had been hampered by the archaic lab equipment, his dullard niece, and the fear of being discovered. The fear nipped at him like a bug, causing him no end of disturbance.

He rolled up Ishara's sleeve, took a cloth swab from the table, and rubbed it into the middle of her arm, leaving a trail of clear liquid.

Returning to the table, he selected a fine syringe, broke the conical head off an ampule, and drew some fluid.

Ishara chose this moment to open her eyes. If she was now aware of what was going on, she did not show it.

Amelia had ignored her uncle's instructions. She stared into the woman's milky grey eyes, eclipsing everything else from her view.

Ishara looked into the little girl's eyes, her face softening.

'Can I touch her? Can I take off the tape, Uncle?'

'Move away from her, Amelia. Do as you're told.'

He injected the fluid into Ishara's forearm. Within seconds, she was unconscious.

Amelia expressed her disappointment with a sigh. 'This is illegal, isn't it? What we're doing? I shouldn't be helping you. If mother and father were to find out, they wouldn't be too happy. First an Outsider and then some old orange Citizen...' She whittled on, squeezing the clear gel onto one of six electro pads he planned to connect to the Avu'lore.

He struck her on the back of the leg with his hand. He had never struck the child before, but having to listen to the girl's squeaky monotone voice for days on end was beginning to wear on him. He hadn't conversed with an adult Citizen in a while — at least not one who was fully conscious.

Amelia screamed, dropping the gel and the pads.

Now I will have to endure a new noise. 'Pick that up! You're in my charge now. I've told you to hold your tongue when I'm doing important work. You do that, or I'll be telling my brother and your precious mother what an insolent daughter they have and be done with it. I've a mind to leave you here tonight. That ought to teach you to obey.'

Amelia picked up the container of gel. Her hand trembled as she retrieved a cloth from the table. She wiped the spilled gel from the floor, dabbing in earnest.

When she had finished wiping the floor, she continued to smear the gel onto the pads. She then gently placed them on either side of the woman's temples, two on her forehead, two on her chest, and the remaining two on her arms.

Her task complete, he shoved his niece aside. He fed two electrode pad wires into the Avu'lore globe. He then inserted the Shards. One would measure the impulses to the brain; the other the heart.

After a short time, the Avu'lore ignited with colour, unveiling specks of yellow, red, blue, green, and purple hues.

He frowned. The globe lacked vivacity. He cupped it in his hands. It felt cold. Dull. Had the Avu'lore lost its power? *No. That can't be it. The electro pads then?* Well-worn and ancient, but all he could acquire.

He heaved a sigh and gazed at the dappled blob which had formed on the screen.

Amelia returned to her chair. Sniffling, she folded her arms and swung her legs.

Skelos waited.

Chapter 21

He stared at the screen for over an hour. After all, he was a scientist and patience went with the territory.

He had to see something this time. Something clearer. His countless experiments, complete with failures and disillusionments, did not dampen his spirits; he simply became more determined to see his investigations through. The fact he had turned to an Outsider proved his determination. For everything there was a price.

He perused a large stock of notes on his handheld tablet, glancing up at the screen at regular intervals. He was exhausted, yet the desire to sleep seldom took him from his work.

Amelia had lost interest in Ishara. She attempted to sleep. She jerked her head up every so often to prevent herself from slipping from her chair.

Another hour passed, and another, until gradually the colours on the screen slowly began to merge. His eyes widened in expectation. One blob seemed to split off from the whole and twist away to one side. As it moved, a shape began to appear — first indistinct but gradually revealing itself to be like that of a hand.

'New? Not witnessed this before.' He spoke his observations aloud into his tablet.

Amelia roused. She sat up. 'Look, Uncle. She's gone pale.'

He saw that Ishara had indeed turned paler than she had been when he had brought her in. Her skin appeared drained of orange blood, save for the orange tinge around her pupils.

'Should I take off the pads?' Amelia was eager to help now. Her uncle looked almost as sickly as the old woman.

'No,' he said, his voice hoarse. He pinched Ishara's wrist, hoping to find some trace of a pulse. He had been so focused on the screen he had failed to monitor her blood pressure. She had flat-lined. The ECG monitor emitted no sound. It displayed a straight line, just as the good doctor told him it would.

He had expected her to last longer than this. True enough, her body was old. But she had a young mind, brimming with knowledge and teeming with mysteries.

He lacked the essential equipment to attempt to revive her, save for his own hands. Having never performed a resuscitation; he did not trust them to do their work.

Better she remains a corpse. He had intended to dispose of her at some point. She was old and given the average life expectancy of a Third Status Citizen was 190, her death would not have been considered suspicious.

He had wanted to fulfil his dream of delving into the human mind, to read it in a catalogue of perfectly formed moving images. Yes, he believed it was possible. It would take time, patience, and determination; all qualities he possessed in abundance. It wasn't too much to desire in the scheme of things.

Finally, he remembered someone had been watching him.

'Have you killed her, Uncle?' said Amelia.

He met his niece's gaze.

And another one I shall have to take care of, he thought bitterly.

Skelos emerged from the cave, leaving Amelia alone with Ishara Molari's body. He felt suffocated by the stagnant air inside the Red Caves and needed a moment to clear his head.

As he walked the tunnel deep in thought, considering how Denlor might aid him in finding another test subject, his footsteps eventually led him to the passage connecting the caves to the surface.

Stepping through, he was greeted by the red dust that blanketed the land. Above it all hovered the telltale shadow of a Citizen airship.

He watched as the vessel drifted by, its passing stirring the dust in swirling currents beneath.

He raced back to his laboratory, his mind a flurry of panic. He stumbled into the cave, his hand on his chest. He had been discovered! He had taken all the precautionary lengths to see to it this wouldn't happen. *How much of this can I explain away?*

Alarmed by his exasperated expression, Amelia jumped from her chair, grasping the hem of her dress. 'What is it, Uncle? What's happened?'

'By-the-Maker, they've found us!'

'How do you know?'

'I just do.' He stripped off his lab coat and flung it to the floor, enraged by his own carelessness. If he had restored the electro-magnetic barrier, they probably would have left. *They'll search every tunnel and cave until they've found every last Outsider and me, my niece, and the body.*

He gave Amelia one of the Shards. 'Keep this for me. Tell no one of it,' he warned her.

Amelia took it from him without saying a word. She understood the urgency. They could both hear them now. The voices. The numerous footsteps.

'Hide it in the folds of your dress,' he told her.

'What is it?'

'Never mind what it is. Just hide it and hide it well.'

Amelia lifted the hem on the side of her dress. She tore a small hole in the seam and slid the Shard through it.

He had to give her credit for her ingeniousness. He slipped the Avu'lore globe into the folds of his robes, hoping it would get lost in the sea of fabric and his layers of fatty tissue.

He crossed to the leaky chamber. A painting sat on top of the mouldy pile. Bright red flowers sprang from the canvas, somehow untouched by the surrounding grime. He lifted one edge of the wooden frame, revealing a narrow gap. *Wide enough.* He pushed the Shard inside and shunted the portion of the frame back into place.

Giddy with panic, he threw his tablet of notes through the hole in the ground and chucked a full bucket of water after it to send it on its way. The tablet held every experiment he had ever done and all his formulas and theories. It was no great loss to him; he could recall most of them by heart.

And then there was the old woman lying on the gurney. Where was he going to hide her? He thought about pushing the gurney into the tunnel. *One strong push and it could go a long way, possibly right through to the other side.*

He heard the synthesized voice of a sentinel cyborg. 'Doctor Skelos Dorm. Do not attempt to flee. We have you surrounded. Do not attempt to flee.'

There was no time to flee, he realised. He would have to cover things up as best he could.

'I think we're caught,' said Amelia, throwing a tray of syringes, tongs, and other instruments through the crack of the floor, along with a flask of sulphuric acid, his Bolt-Shot Whip, and the laser gun he had set down on the ledge.

'Not those, you stupid girl!'

'Sorry, Uncle.' She threw more utensils through the crack, whatever she could find small enough to fit.

They were seconds away now.

He wrapped Ishara's body in a white sheet and dragged her off the gurney onto the floor. He then hauled it into the cupboard under the work table and hurriedly slid the doors shut.

Amelia returned to her chair. Her eyes wide with guilt and fright.

A host of Citizen guards marched in. They were joined by Kerss Nysen, a director on the board of the Pareus Scientific Research and Funding Division, Osaphar, and a man wearing the Planetary Protection Committee shields. Skelos had seen him in his former Stores once or twice but did not know his name.

This is suitably awkward. Skelos couldn't have been less pleased to see his former best friend. Osaphar gave him a stiff glance of recognition. Skelos smiled back.

He wondered if Osaphar had betrayed him by leading Kerss and the others to the Red Caves. Osaphar knew him too well. He couldn't make an enemy of his old friend; he had too much to lose.

Kerss stared around the cave. 'What are you doing here, Skelos?'

'Exploring.'

'Exploring what?' Her prying eyes darted around, taking in every detail.

He heard a scratching sound outside. *There must be more of them waiting. They've come to take me away.*

'It is quite clear you are conducting experiments,' Kerss said. 'To have come all the way out here, you must be desperate.'

What was the use in denying it when he was surrounded by the evidence? 'How did you find me?' He glanced at Osaphar. *If he wants to renew our friendship – then he should do it at the appropriate time and in the appropriate manner.*

'No matter.' She motioned one of the guards over. 'Search the premises. Leave that place until last.' She told a guard who had lurched towards the leaky ante-chamber. 'It will probably be quite anti-climactic once we've waded through this lot.'

Skelos and Amelia stood in one corner watching as they conducted their search.

The guards sifted through beakers and ampules using scanning wands with laser tips to detect banned substances. They found traces of prohibited items on all the equipment Skee had brought and some Denlor had acquired. The guards seemed to enjoy knocking most instruments onto the ground, smashing containers and glass. The shattered remains filled his ears.

The guards did a thorough search. Kerss had taken a wand herself, tapping it on a gurney and stabbing its wheels with her boot heel. She ran it along a worktable before crouching under to check for anything hidden.

Skelos swallowed.

'What's this?' said Kerss, tugging at the white sheet trailing from the table's storage cabinet. The door creaked open and the old woman's corpse slid out.

She screamed and jumped back in horror. The body hit the floor: a tangle of grey hair and skin like bleached bone.

Kerss soon composed herself. She stooped down and pulled the rest of the sheet away from the body. She stared into the sunken pale face of Ishara Molari. She lifted the corpse's right hand, examined it, and then let it drop. 'One of our own,' she said through clenched teeth.

'It's not what you think,' said Skelos,' his voice calm and condoning. 'She was a willing subject, but old.' He pointed to the gurney. 'She died right there on the table.'

'It's true,' said Amelia, taking her uncle's hand. 'It was an accidental experiment.'

Skelos snapped Amelia's hand back with his own. 'Shut up,' he hissed.

Amelia quietly rubbed her wrist.

Kerss shook her head and frowned at the little girl. 'And to think a child has been witness to all...all this. It is clear to me you have not learned your lesson, Dr Dorm.'

She instructed a broad-shouldered guard to remove Ishara's body. The guard wrapped the corpse in the sheet. He hefted it over his shoulder and took it out to the ship.

Another two guards began loading the prohibited items into metal crates. In essence, they were loading everything. They gathered as much as they could in their gloved-hands and tossed it into the crates as if it was worth nothing, which it most likely was since most of it was damaged or broken.

'We'll take all of this as evidence,' said Kerss. 'What about your files and formulas? And we'll need a list of your subjects.'

'Why would I hand that information over to you?' said Skelos. He tapped his forehead. 'It's all in here. Perhaps if you allowed me to complete my work, you'd have been able to extract that information for yourself.'

Kerss gave him a thin smile. She removed a metal case from under her arm and placed it on the table with a dull thud. Flicking the latches open, she revealed an electronic syringe nestled inside. The drug it contained, called Axiom, was the closest thing the Establishment had developed to a truth serum. Its effects would leave patients in a foggy, confused state, likely to divulge anything. Skelos was adamant that no amount of drugs could loosen his tongue — he had too many secrets, too many for the Establishment to ever know.

'No need for that,' said Osaphar, taking the syringe out of Kerss's hands. 'We know his experiments failed. And we do not need to do this in front of the child. He'll have files in his old Stores or in his home. We shall look there. And if we can't find them, so be it. There is no place for such research on this planet.'

Kerss nodded. 'Very well.' She stared into the leaky chamber. 'What's through there?'

A guard stalked over to the antechamber and prodded at some remnants of mouldy fabric with his detector probe.

'That's all mine,' said Skelos. The painting in which he had hidden the Shard sat right on top of the mound in plain sight. 'All of it. Don't touch it. Careful.'

The guard lifted the fading piece of artwork, pursing his lips at the foul odour. 'It reeks in here.'

Skelos snatched the painting out of his hands. 'You insult me. This has been in my family for centuries.'

'Clear this lot out,' Kerss informed the guard. 'Let's see what else you're hiding.'

Chapter 22

Skelos didn't notice the guards gathering outside the ante-chamber in their face masks and goggles. All he saw were the scraps of debris and junk coming out of it.

He had set the painting to one side and was trying to avert his gaze from Osaphar, whose obstinate stare was causing him some discomfort, when they dragged the body out by its arm. It was the bare-chested Greasy-Haired One who had slit his own throat. The wound was caked in blood and debris, but it gaped down to the bone.

Skelos choked back a gasp. He had barely warmed to his surroundings, if that were possible, and now all this.

'An Outsider,' said one of the guards, examining the corpse's hand. 'His throat has been slit.'

'A half-wit can see his throat has been slit,' said Skelos. 'I didn't do it. An autopsy will confirm it.' *What are you saying, you fool? He's an Outsider. They wouldn't care if you slit his throat or not.*

He could not help but wonder if the Hooded Man had planted the body in the ante-chamber on purpose. Given the multitude of tunnels and caves in the vicinity, it seemed too great a coincidence.

'An autopsy may confirm some anomalies, I'm sure,' said Kerss. 'However, I think the atrocity you have created here is enough for us to concede that your time in Odisiris has come to an end.'

'An end?' *He squeezed his niece's hand. They're going to kill me. Right here in the Red Caves in front of Amelia – in front of my former friend.* 'Me, meaning?'

'Meaning you are to be exiled,' said Osaphar.

'Exiled?' Skelos had heard of tales of exiles. Tales that exile was worse than torture – than death. But as no exiled Citizen had ever returned to Odisiris; such tales could not be corroborated. Crimes were punishable by exile or death. But there was little crime in Odisiris.

Sentinel cyborgs ensured acts of violence were rare. Murders were scarce. As Citizens had the ability to self-heal, acts of abduction were favoured among the criminally minded. The justice system was swift, and no criminal trials were ever publicised.

'You can't exile me for this,' said Skelos. 'Ishara Molari was coming to the end of her years. She was half dead when I met her. She knew this and, hence, she was a willing subject. More than willing in fact, she begged me. Tell them Amelia.'

'You used the cords to restrain her,' said a guard, holding the frayed ropes in his hand. Frayed from the old woman trying to gnaw her way through them.

'It's true,' Amelia piped up, although a little late. 'She asked to be part of it, rather kindly. She said she always wanted to be experimented on. She didn't mind being cut open or anything.'

Skelos gave Amelia's hand a quick jerk for her alluded confession.

'You were carrying out unlawful experiments on Citizens,' said Kerss. 'Do you have proof that she gave her consent?'

She had given a consent of sorts. He had asked Ishara if she would help him and she had said, 'Yes, if I can.' She never asked what help he required. 'Her word,' said Skelos.

'Her *word* won't help you,' said Osaphar. 'We have no choice but to exile you to another planet.'

'On whose authority?' Skelos's eyes darted accusingly between Kerss and Osaphar. He was certain the decree regarding his exile hadn't come from either one of them.

'The Parliamentary Elite,' said Kerss.

The Establishment consisted of three of Odisiris's major powers: the Parliamentary Elite, the Planetary Data Protection Committee, and the Pareus Scientific Research and Funding Division.

Skelos guided Amelia over to the chair and placed his hand firmly on her shoulder, pushing her down onto the seat. He rolled up the sleeves of his robes. 'I wish to converse with them at once.'

Osaphar shook his head. 'The decision has already been made. You will go there now.'

'I deserve a hearing.' He shoved Amelia out of the chair and plonked himself down. 'It's my right as a Citizen.'

Kerss and Osaphar exchanged a furtive glance.

What are they hiding? Whether they found Ishara here or not, it would appear that the Establishment had sealed his fate.

'You lost your right as a Citizen when you carried out this disgusting act on your race,' said Kerss. She tucked her syringe case under her arm. 'There will be no trial for you, Skelos Dorm.'

'I can't leave my niece,' he replied, mercilessly squeezing Amelia's hand. 'There is no one to take care of her.'

'She can go with you,' said Kerss. 'You can take a few luxury items as well.' Her eyes roamed the cave in search of something one might deem a luxury. 'You must leave everything else behind.'

'I don't have any luxury items, except for this.' Skelos grasped the painting. He silently cursed Amelia for throwing his Bolt-Shot Whip away. It had belonged to his father and held some sentimental value. 'And this.' He pointed to the ancient microscope.

'You're welcome to that stinking piece of mould,' said a guard.

'I'd like a word with Skelos alone,' said Osaphar, turning to Kerss. 'I shall meet you on the ship. Take Amelia with you.'

Kerss took Amelia's hand and waved the remaining guards out. Amelia looked back at him. Skelos wondered if Kerss would dare use the Axiom serum on his niece. It would have been a waste, of course. Prompted with the right questions, Amelia would provide the answers, albeit not in the promptness or order that Kerss would no doubt like.

Not until their footsteps became dull echoes in the tunnel did Osaphar speak. 'You cannot run from this, Skelos.'

'What makes you think I would run?' He smirked at the suggestion. It wasn't a question of if he would run, it was a question of when. Waiting until board the ship offered a clean getaway, allowing him to discreetly disable launch. Alternatively, compromising one of the robot guards could prove useful for seizing control of the situation. As a wanted man, remaining on Odisiris was no longer an option. The ship would deliver him to his vault, well-stocked for on-the-run provisions and supplies. From there, a brief stop at his residence would complete preparations before disappearing without a trace.

'Because you have the advantage, and I know you too well.'

'What advantage is that?'

'I know of your Gift. I witnessed it first-hand on the most daring adventure we ever took as children,' he stared around, and then his eyes settled on him once more, and they were colder than they had ever been, 'to this place. And yet we claim not to believe in magic.' He raised an eyebrow. 'I wouldn't attempt to hijack a ship if I were you.'

'Do you think me witless?' he spat. 'It never entered my head to escape. I have my niece to think about.'

He had always gone to great lengths to conceal his talents with technology from all but his closest family. Even they did not know the full extent of his abilities. He made especially sure that his ex-wife never discovered this secret side of him.

He couldn't know. He's only guessing. My Gift does not simply reveal itself. 'Surely, you're not going to let them exile me. Can't you talk to them?'

'I don't have a choice as you know. I am not one of the Establishment, nor will I ever be.' Osaphar leaned on the wall. 'It's very difficult to keep secrets when you're young. You always find you must tell someone.'

He's bluffing. He knows nothing. 'We have left our childhood behind us, and we have – I hope – evolved. I trust you are not burdening yourself with any misconstrued events you witnessed as a child. We all have secrets. I trust you kept mine as I have kept yours.'

Osaphar gave him a hard stare. 'The world we are going to is Narrigh,' he said after some quiet reflection.

'It's different from here. Given time, you will appreciate it. It's an improvement on where we are now.'

'You say we?'

'Yes. I too have made Narrigh my home.'

'You are also to be exiled?' His declaration made Skelos feel a little better. Old friends reacquainted.

'It's a choice for me, an exile for you.'

Skelos thought of what he was leaving behind, and panic shook him. 'What will become of me there? All my worldly possessions are here. I need to get items from my vault.'

'No. You will take nothing more with you. As to what is to become of you, you will be doing what you love most – experiments. You'll never have another opportunity as great as this.'

Skelos thought he saw a glint in Osaphar's eyes.

He gave him a knowing smile. 'I understand perfectly. You needn't say more. How foolish of him. This wasn't an exile. The Establishment was simply transporting him to another planet where there would be Stores big enough for him to continue his work with more compliant participants. They had seen the value of his research, after all. Kerss had obviously been trying to procure his formulas for herself before they took off – so to speak. He imagined the Establishment was divided over whether his experiments were ethical.

He vowed to keep his formulas to himself. They were stored away in his head, ready to spill out when needed. *Out with the old world and in with the new.* 'So, when do we leave?'

Chapter 23

As Skelos emerged from the Red Caves, he paused to take in the swirling red dust that seemed suspended in the air.

Beyond the familiar transport they had arrived on, a hulking new vessel sat grounded. He hadn't been on many vessels like this one before. It dwarfed their ship. Panels and antennas studded its surface, hints at the advanced technology it contained within.

A smaller airship took off, sending the red dust into a frenzy. Skelos covered his nose and mouth with the sleeve of his robe. Everyone else had already boarded for departure.

Before him lay an open boarding ramp, extended like a long silver tongue beckoning him inside. 'What ship is this?' he asked.

'The *Engardia*,' said Osaphar. 'And this is where I say goodbye.'

'You said you were coming with me?' He was suddenly terrified. Up until now, he had always considered himself to be resourceful and independent. He was going to a planet he had never heard of with no one for company but his insolent niece. He would have to make new friends and acquaintances all by himself without Osaphar's guidance and support.

'I believe I said we were bound for the same place,' said Osaphar with a thin smile. 'I cannot travel with you to Narrigh today. But I'm sure our paths will cross in Narrigh at some point in time.'

Skelos gave a weighty sigh as the guard escorted him up the boarding ramp.

There was no need to panic. He would meet Osaphar at a later date. He would cordially invite him for dinner when he had settled into this new home. All was not lost. Osaphar had smiled at him. And he didn't smile often. *He wants to renew our friendship.* It was impossible with the Establishment in the way. It wouldn't help Osaphar's status to be associated with a failed scientist and the former wife of a member of the Parliamentary Elite.

He was slightly discomfited by the fact that Osaphar hadn't introduced him to the ship's captain, and he was forced to walk the ship in search of him. He eventually found a sphere droid to direct him to the cockpit. The droid bobbed and floated along, guiding him through the ship's galley. It took him past a teleportation platform, hidden structures encased in metal, and then through the cockpit entryway.

The crew did not turn around when he entered. They remained at their workstations. He had to cough loudly to finally catch the captain's attention. It seemed the man already knew he was there but chose not to acknowledge him.

'Dr Skelos!' said the captain, extending an arm and striding to meet him, all legs, teeth and boyish looks. His long torso was clad in light armour. On his breast, a mosaic badge marked his rank—a geometric design of interlocking cubes. His right arm displayed a line of etched crests running from wrist to shoulder. 'Welcome, Captain Badone at your service. Magnificent, isn't it?'

Skelos wondered what was so magnificent. They hadn't gone anywhere yet. 'How long will it take to reach Narrigh?'

'Not long,' replied Badone, 'but the ride can get bumpy. 'It will be smoother if you're hyper-sleep.'

'Not me,' said Skelos. He wanted to stay awake for the entire journey. Have a good poke about, find out more about this Narrigh and the work expected of him. 'You could put Amelia to sleep. If she's not asleep already.' He looked around but could not see her. 'It would be a wise decision. She's easily frightened.'

Badone nodded. 'Then it shall be done.'

He sauntered over to the far end of the deck. A large rotating globe sat on top of the pedestal. He placed his hand on the globe, and the upper hemisphere swung upwards, unveiling an array of bottles and glasses.

'Zaskian or Primnicott?' he said.

'Zaskian,' said Skelos.

Badone poured a clear liquid from one of the bottles into a tall glass. For himself, he poured an amber-colored liquid. Leaving the globe ajar, he brought over the two drinks.

This was more like it. Osaphar has seen to it that he would be well treated, that there would be no humiliation to be had with exile. He wondered now if his deportation was only temporary. Once he had perfected his work, he expected that Odisiris would want him back. But would he go back? If he found Narrigh to his liking, he would of course stay, and Odisiris would be nothing but another holiday destination.

He took the glass of Zaskian from Badone. 'This isn't what I was expecting,' he said

'What were you expecting — exactly? Did you expect us to lock you away, humiliate you in front of your niece, tie you up, and knock you out? You're a

First Status Citizen doctor, and you will be treated as such.'

Badone tapped Skelos's glass with his own, and together they drained their glasses.

The Zaskian was a dry and potent brew. Skelos had not drank it in a while and was overcome by a sudden lightheadedness. The captain's face became a blur, the ship's windows a shadow.

He needed to sit down. He stumbled over to the railings. The glass slipped from his hand, shattering on the floor; he joined it two seconds later.

Chapter 24

Skelos woke on a wooden bench. In Odisiris, wood was an uncommon material for interior furnishing. For one preposterous moment, he thought he was in a garden. Except, he felt no fresh air above his head. The smell of fresh leaves did not waft up his nose. But he did note an odd, almost unidentifiable, smell. He sniffed under one of his armpits to ensure the smell did not come from him. It had been a while since he had bathed.

All around him were rough-hewn walls of grey rock, rising up into an uneven ceiling pockmarked with age. Across from where he sat, a heavy wooden door was set within an arched stone frame. Both door and frame showed signs of years of use. Scuff marks ran along the bottom of the wood, and the stone around it had been worn smooth in places.

Very strange.

He massaged his temples. He must have drunk too much Zaskian. There was a jug of water, and a small glass set on a table beside the bench. Thank the Palm-of-his-Maker; he was parched.

He drank directly from the jug and wiped his mouth. An open archway at the far side of the room revealed nothing but darkness beyond. The sparse furnishings—a tall, narrow table, a single chair, a wardrobe, and a chest of drawers—were all made from the same rough-hewn wood. Is that what he could smell: bark?

With a sigh, he cast his eyes around the small space once more, unimpressed. He would make a complaint about his treatment when he was more settled. If this was Narrigh, where was the welcoming committee?

Where was his laboratory and his new abode? *Surely this can't be it.* And furthermore, where was Amelia?

He approached the heavy wooden door, grasping the ornate iron knocker that was fixed in place. No sound came as he rattled it. Frustrated, he ran his hand along the rough stone wall, hoping to find a hidden security panel. After several seconds of searching, he dropped his arm in confusion.

He shouted in his loudest voice for attention. Moments later, the door creaked open to reveal a stern-faced woman. Her sharp brown eyes studied him from behind a long, straight nose. A crumpled, embroidered gown was draped over her thin frame, the high collar trimmed with golden threads. Heavy rings, encrusted with dull gemstones, adorned each of her slender fingers. Without a word, she pulled the door shut behind her.

Shocked by the vulgarity of her attire and the way in which she sauntered right up to him, inches from his face, without standing at the door waiting to be summoned, without humility or qualm, Skelos took a while to find his voice. 'Who-who are you?'

'Halera Proth. And you are Mr Scolos Dim.'

'*Doctor* Skelos Dorm,' he snapped. *They haven't even taken the time to get my name right.* 'This is an insult. How dare you lock me up like this? Where is Captain Badone? I wish to speak with him at once. Where is my niece? Why are my—'

He ran his hands over his clothes, checking each pocket and fold of fabric. His fingers brushed against the small bump in his jacket lining. His Worral Stone, a precious Gift token, was still safely tucked away near his chest. But as he patted other parts of his attire, he felt significantly lighter. Too light. Reaching inside himself, he searched for the familiar tug of the Avu'lore globe. But he found only emptiness where it had been. The Shard was also gone. Stolen!

Helara bit her lip. 'Your possessions are under your bed.'

'Bed? What's the matter with you? There is no bed in here.'

Halera pointed to the wooden bench on which he had woken. It had a fat pillow at one end and some fluffy rag that might have been a blanket.

'*That* is not my bed,' he hissed through his teeth. He passed her a scathing look before hefting up his robes and getting on his hands and knees. He plunged his arm under the bench. His fingers found the Avu'lore globe, but the painting and the Shard were gone. He cranked himself to his feet, his face blue with rage.

'Explain yourself,' he demanded of Halera. 'I am a renowned scientist and Citizen of the highest rank. How dare you greet me so casually?' The memories swirling in his aching head told of accepting a drink from a ship's captain, and nothing thereafter.

'Osaphar said you might be difficult and that it may take you a while to adapt to your new home. Of course, if this room is not to your liking, I can allocate you another one more spacious. I apologise if there has been any misunderstanding.'

That was more like it. They had some nerve allocating him the servants' quarters in the first place. He made a mental note of his complaints thus far. It was bad enough they hadn't allowed him to bring a change of clothes, but they had also stolen his loot. This was catastrophic. 'There has been a colossal misunderstanding. See to it that my possessions are returned, and my niece is brought to me at once.'

'I'm one of the Shardner government councillors, or ministers, if you prefer. You will be working for us. You will take all your orders from us. The Shardner govern all of Narrigh, some regions better than others. Our offices are in the Royal Halls, in the Kingdom of Baruch. You will be expected to abide by Narrigh traditions and embrace the Baruchian culture.'

He wasn't sure if he heard correctly. 'Bar-bar...what?' His attempt at speaking caught in his parched throat. After draining several gulps from the water jug, he took a long breath. Clearing his throat, he focused on each syllable, trying again to communicate what he needed. 'Orders? I have no intention of taking orders from you. What Status are you? What's the name of your House?'

'Status? I'm not one of your kind. I do not have a mark, Dr Dim.' She raised both her palms.

No, there is no Mark, thought Skelos. His knees buckled and darkness swallowed him as he collapsed to the floor.

Chapter 25

Skelos opened his eyes, greeted by soft fabric under his head. He took a deep breath, breathing in the fresh scent of outdoors still lingering on the pillow.

He lifted his head and eased himself to the edge of the stone bed where there sat a low table, set with a thick leather-bound book. He picked it up and sniffed the pages. Paper was a rare commodity in Odisiris, and he hadn't seen any for a long time. The book had a gold cross on the front of it. He flicked through the pages. From what he could make out, the book was about some ancient deity. He had read about other races and their gods when he was a boy. He didn't find it very interesting. Though people had to believe in something he supposed.

He swung his legs over the edge of the bed, closed his eyes, and pressed the heels of his hands to his temples as he recalled his unfortunate dream, the one where he had awoken in a small room and was greeted by an Unmarked One who claimed to be one of those in charge.

He laughed. 'How silly.' What was not silly was how he had been denied quarters befitting of his Status. He would have expected Osaphar to see to it that he had all his home comforts.

He entered the open archway and found himself in a small washroom. Against one wall sat an old cast iron bathtub, its surface worn from years of use. In the corner was a wooden box with a hinged lid—he guessed it must be the toilet, as there was nothing else that could serve that purpose.

A small square door on the opposite side of the room led out to a narrow balcony. The stone railing showed signs of weathering from many seasons of wind and rain. Exhausted and unsteady on his feet, he stumbled forward and grasped the railing for support. Leaning over, he was stunned by how high up he was. Below stretched lush green hills dotted with trees, and a winding dirt path that disappeared into the dense forest in the distance.

Beyond the forest, a steep cliff rose sharply towards the sky. Perched at the top was a gleaming white city, its golden domes and towers visible even from so far away. Colourful banners and flags fluttered in the breeze. Such a beautiful city. He wondered why he was not in it.

The sound of footsteps drew him back inside. The woman was there again, the woman from his dream. She stood in the washroom in a grey robe, not as crumpled as the last, but hideous nonetheless with its stiff collar and bulbous shoulder pads. *Am I dreaming?*

His eyes narrowed as she blocked his path. 'Stay away from me,' he growled, finger raised in warning. To avoid even accidental contact, he nearly stumbled into the iron tub behind him in his haste to squeeze past. Nothing of his simple robe would touch anything of hers. Did exile mean losing everything—rank, title, even basic dignity? All that remained was this cold cell and unwanted questions. He squeezed past her and sought refuge on his stone bed. 'Where's the captain? Where's Osaphar?'

Helara followed him. 'Do you like your new quarters?' She crossed her arms. 'I know this is a huge adjustment for you, Mr Dim, but you have been exiled.

Exiled Citizens hold no rank here. You will be working for the Shardner. We have a specific line of work which we believe suits your field. We will take care of your niece. We'll let you settle in, and then we shall send for you.' With that, she took her leave, closing off his last hope.

Alone at last, he curled tight upon the bare stone bed, tears coming as sleep finally took him.

Chapter 26

The next morning Skelos was resolute: he would escape. He hadn't thought beyond the stone- walled chamber, of how and when he might secure a ship out of Narrigh. But that was his plan, nonetheless.

Each knock brought a new opportunity. His first attempt as an escapee was somewhat embarrassing. He scampered to the corner of the ceiling by the door and hung there like a spider waiting for an unsuspecting fly.

He launched from his perch onto the wary servant below, knocking him unconscious. He then hurled himself down the first few steps of a winding staircase. He never saw the end of the staircase that day. He was greeted by a guard with a baton who whacked him hard in the stomach and chopped his hand in the back of his head, knocking him onto the tiles and out cold. When he awoke, he found himself back in his stone-walled chamber.

His lack of fortitude surprised him. It was most un-Citizen like. Where was the planning, the care, that defined a true Citizen?

Despite the extra padding of fat around his middle, he could not make himself comfortable on a bed made of stone. He spent most nights awake. The food they served him was plain and the portions small. It would help if he knew where he was and what he would be escaping to. He felt as if he was light years away from the home that rejected him, oh so coldly.

He rubbed his hands together and stared around his poor surroundings. He found himself missing Amelia and her incessant questions, her insolence, and the hideous dresses she insisted on wearing.

He had always imagined exiled Citizens were sent to other planets within the galaxy with similar cultures and traditions to their own. Given his Status, he wasn't expecting this – mistreatment.

There came a knock on the door. He had become accustomed to the knocks: a weak one for the servants, a strong one for the guards, and no knocks for members of the Shardner.

'Yes, filth.' Despite loathing anyone who walked through the door, he welcomed the interruptions. It broke up the day and lifted his mood. Hurling insults at Unmarked Ones became his guiltless pleasure.

The servant, a young man with a hunched back and stumpy legs, entered carrying a clean towel over his arm and a jug of water. He placed the water and the towel on the table and left without a word. Only members of the so-called Shardner spoke to him. He guessed the others had been instructed not to communicate. Not that he wanted to get into the habit of conversing with Unmarked Ones; he would sooner eat his own tongue. He was thinking he might have to when one of the Shardner came through the door.

A grey-bearded man entered, cloak swirling. He closed the door behind him and gave a throaty growl.

'Skelos. How are you? Are they treating you well?' His words were warm, but his eyes were cold and uncaring. *He stands by the door as if I and my living quarters are more than he can bear.*

'What do you want?'

The man whipped his cloak behind him. Beneath it he wore a worn shirt and trousers. Heavy boots encased his feet. 'My name is Yerryn Denvor. I've been made to understand that you feel you have been duped?'

'Understand from whom?'

'From the Shardner council and the servants.'

'So, you have them spying on me as well. This exile is unjust. No one has given me a nuance of respect. I'm being starved to death by your deplorable food. The air smells foul. I have the right to relocated as per Odisirian law.' He was a little hazy on the details of the Odisirian law concerning exile, having never been exiled before. In fact, he had never been involved in the Odisirian legal system or politics; he had always relied on Nylthia for that.

'That law was amended under the new vice-chancellor. Unless Narrigh is on the brink of ruin, you cannot request a transfer.'

'And what would you know about it?' He seized his pitcher of water and took a long drink, hoping it would take the edge off his hunger.

'I know your people. I'm a Peltarck.'

Skelos wiped the water from under his chin and set down the empty jug. It wasn't the first time he had come across a Peltarck. Peltarcks came from the planet Pyridian within the Andromeda Galaxy.

'How did you find your way here?'

'I was asked to come here as penance for a crime I committed long ago.'

'And they made you a member of this Shardner government?'

'I obtained this position through hard work. I started as a secretary for Sahara, one of the other council members. She appreciated my skills as an advisory and promoted me.'

'How long did that take?'

'Eleven years. Given time, you too could be placed in a position of trust.'

Skelos was not about to wait eleven years to attain a high position on a planet ruled by Unmarked Ones. The very thought of it produced a strange cloying sensation in his stomach. 'You're Peltarck. I'm Citizen. Perhaps your idea of a position of trust is different from mine. The very fact that there put me on this despicable planet is a testimony to the position of trust the Parliamentary Elite have bestowed on me. They will never trust me. And rightly so; I do not trust them. I expect that being in Narrigh is a life of luxury compared to Pyridian. Why you get to see a real sunrise and sunset every day.'

The Peltarck smiled. 'Mock if you will. Narrigh takes some getting used to. One day you may have the chance to invent something new here, and you will be well rewarded for it.'

'But I don't want to invent something new here for Outsiders to benefit.'

'We are the *outsiders* here. You must refrain from using that term. It will not be welcome. Unmarked is the correct term for non-Citizens as you and I well know.'

'Outcast perhaps,' Skelos mumbled, 'but I will never be an outsider. 'Granted the Unmarked Ones here are not the same as the breed I have come across on Odisiris, still I do not see why they should profit from my expertise.'

'You work for the Shardner now Skelos, not yourself. Forget about your own needs for the time being. You will be watched, and you will be expected to carry out the tasks assigned to you. We will tell you when to wake, and when to sleep. Your days will be busy. If you cooperate, I will help you learn about this new world you are in. If you comply, I will show you a little of it.'

He knew the Peltarck was right and he spoke the truth. He supposed he could pretend to comply while focusing on a more sophisticated escape plan. There had to be ships from Odisiris landing in Narrigh all the time. He would steal one.

Chapter 27

The following day, Skelos woke from another restless night. He climbed over the balcony railing to grab the tree branch growing out of the cliffside where his humble quarters were situated. The wood cracked under his weight, sending him falling with a terrified scream. A servant and two guards rushed over to rescue him. They lifted him back onto the patio. He lashed out at them. They took the full brunt of his frustration and his disgust. They were all Unmarked. And they had touched him. Contaminated him.

He sat in his bath and scrubbed his flesh until it was raw. Logic told him he was acting like a fool, but his Citizen Status told him that all Unmarked Ones were disgusting, germ carrying beings, with no communication skills or etiquette. And yet he could see with his own eyes that these Unmarked Ones were different. They were polite. Firm but polite. They had no problems communicating with him, and they were clean.

He staggered from the bath and wrapped his – now – very blue skin in a towel. He stepped out of the bath shaking his head. Why would they send him here? He didn't understand it. He thought about how he could make a less rash escape. He began scheming ways to negotiate leaving this "nightmare of a planet," though had no clues on Amelia's location to use as an excuse. He wondered whether she was in Narrigh. She could still be on Odisiris, facing a drilling under Kerss's stern gaze with the Axiom drug running through what was left of her veins.

That night he slept soundly given the day's traumas, and the next day he woke fresh and more rational-minded. One of the servants had laid out a black lab coat for him. He slipped it on.

Sitting on the bed while flipping through the Bible, he was interrupted by Yerryn arriving with four armed guards in leather tunics, tough cotton breeches and brown boots. Without greeting, they guided him downstairs and outside to a grassy area overlooking a red dirt path. There stood a stocky workhorse hitched to an open wooden cart, attended by a lean man with pointed ears.

Skelos followed them down the winding staircase lit by sconces. He was not looking forward to his next destination but was glad to be finally free of his room, if only for a brief time.

A lean man with pointed ears and a jaw set like a trap held the leather reins were strapped to the mighty animal. He wore a shabby cloak, a rich embroidered tunic, and oil skin trousers.

'What is this?' said Skelos.

'It's a horse and cart,' said Yerryn. 'And this is Ryelm.' He gestured to the man with the pointed ears. 'He will take us into the heart of Baruch. The Kingdom.'

Ryelm gave no greeting, simply directing the horse into turning the cart to face them.

'I don't understand this horse and cart,' said Skelos. The animal seemed docile, and the cart as fragile as glass.

'You sit in the cart,' said the guard, tapping the side of the wooden structure, and the horse will pull you. We'll be in the kingdom by nightfall.'

Skelos laughed. This had to be a cruel joke. He looked up at the sky. Small-winged birds circled. 'Can we not take an airship?'

'There are no airships here,' said Yerryn. 'Odisirian vessels do not belong in Narrigh.'

Skelos attempted to climb into the cart without jumping, a feat he would have found impossible if one of the guards hadn't taken the liberty of shoving him in the rump.

Yerryn climbed in next, followed by three guards who squeezed in beside them. That left little room to move.

Up front, Ryelm swung himself into the driver's seat. With a click of his tongue, he snapped the reins. The horse broke into a plodding trot. The cart trundled and creaked along.

Skelos gripped the rough wooden sides, complaining inwardly that he could have walked faster.

Chapter 28

Skelos had been enamored by the Kingdom when he had viewed it from his balcony. But within its walls, the reality was very different.

Baruch was dusty and busy.

Horses and carts packed the streets. Skelos saw a whole plethora of species that he had never laid eyes upon. Repugnant scents assaulted his senses—scented oils, sweat, overripe fruit and rancid meat mingled on the breeze. He cupped his hands over his nose and mouth to block out the worst of the smells.

Yerryn didn't seemed bothered by the rancid smells or the hectic atmosphere. Few of the populace greeted the Peltarck with words or a smile.

Skelos and Yerryn walked ahead as Ryelm trailed behind them. From what Skelos could tell the Peltarck did not seem to care for Ryelm's company. Yerryn ignored the man's attempt at trivial conversation regarding their walking route. After which, Ryelm did not speak.

From Skelos's view, the Peltarck cared little for Ryelm's company, ignoring his attempts at idle chatter about their path. Afterward, Ryelm said no more. Skelos found Ryelm's flowery perfume overpowering, causing his eyes to water. The Peltarck's company he could at least tolerate, the smells he could not.

Guards flanked them—one ahead, two behind. One guard, a Citizen of the Third Class, pulled on dark gloves to hide the orange mark on his hand. He paid Skelos no mind.

He knew better than to flee in this unfamiliar land without learning its ways. The buildings were made of stone, some white and some decorated with gold, though he couldn't say if it was real. Unlike his homeland, they offered little ventilation in the heat.

The difference between the poor and the rich was clearly marked. The Kingdom bustled with many street urchins dressed in threadbare clothes while the wealthy strutted about in lavishly coloured robes. In Odisiris it was not so. Anyone living on Odisiris had wealth, some more than others. Odisiris, all enjoyed prosperity, except the subhuman Outsiders in the Red Caves and those on Brevons Beach.

'They do not bow here?' Skelos whispered in the Peltarck's ear.

'There was a king and queen who ruled here once. The people bowed to them. They died many years ago.'

Skelos found this intriguing. Most of the known planets in the Andromeda Galaxy had presidents, commanders, and ruling chancellors as their leaders; a few had emperors, but none a king and queen.

'Who commands you all?' asked Skelos.

'I don't understand the question,' said Yerryn.

'Who is the main ruler? Who makes all the real decisions?'

'We are a democracy. Decisions rest on all our shoulders. Although, if you were to ask me, I would say that Ilvis is the more dominate Shardner member among us, and the oldest. He is most respected.'

'And what of outside the Kingdom of Baruch?'

Yerryn stopped walking and turned to him. 'You do understand that you cannot travel outside the Kingdom?'

Skelos did not think his question unreasonable. He did not see why his exile should stretch no further than the Kingdom of Baruch. He had the right to see the rest of it as far as he was concerned. It was the surest way to plan his fail-safe escape plan. 'And why not?'

'It is forbidden for races who are not of this world to leave the Kingdom. I brought you out here to show you some courtesy before your real undertaking begins and to teach you a little about Narrigh's culture.'

Skelos wasn't sure that he cared to learn about Narrigh's culture — it being very different than his own.

They came to a building of solid stone.

Skelos climbed down from the cart, wrestling the guard who attempted to help him. He followed Yerryn into a lavishly furnished hall, too lavish for his liking, too busy and too colourful. The mosaic crammed floor made his head swim. The walls were a parade of vertical green, purple, gold, and black stripes. The gilded framed chairs were upholstered in a garish yellow and blue floral fabric. The glossy wood furniture stood on slender carved legs, and the paintings on the wall were so full of colour they were barely distinguishable amidst the eye-popping wallpaper. A huge table ran down the length of the room. Covered in a green velvet cloth with a tasseled trim, it was laden with several bowls of oversized fruit. The fruit looked as if it was coated with wax — or made from it, he surmised.

Skelos saw one face he recognized, and it was not Osaphar. It was the woman who had first greeted him in Narrigh, the Unmarked One: Halera Proth.

The large table had space for twelve people to sit, though only nine were currently occupying chairs. Halera motioned for Skelos to take one of the empty seats. She sat at the head of the table; her neck wrapped in animal fur.

He remained standing. Of all the Unmarked Ones he had encountered so far, Halera repulsed him the most with her messy hair, worn clothes, and twisted smile.

The other eight studying him with careful gazes.

Yerryn sat down, breaking the silence.

He fiddled with the buttons on his black coat. He was certain not one of the twelve council members bore a Mark. He did not belong among them. The outsider. The alien. None rose in greeting or offered a welcoming smile. Instead, his eyes rested on a decorative bowl of wax fruit. They had stranded him on a planet teeming with Unmarked Ones. Who knew how many more were out there?

'Change can be challenging, Mr Dorm,' said a large man with a face full of freckles and gold rings upon his fingers. 'I can imagine things are a little different here than on your home planet.'

Does he not know how to pronounce the word doctor?

'You will work alone. Guarded of course,' said Yerryn, helping himself to a bunch of purple grapes. 'You will work and sleep in one of our underground chambers. At the weekends you can return to your quarters if you wish, or you can stay here.'

Skelos raised his chin, his eyes skimmed the nine now seated at the table: mature men and women: dark, pale, large, small. All hostile. 'This is an outrage. I was told nothing about this? Where is Osaphar? I didn't come here to work for the likes of you.'

As far as he knew, expatriates didn't work. They were sent away to live a luxurious lifestyle elsewhere, not to slave.

'Sit down, Skelos,' said the large man. His meaty hand flapped, urging him to the chair. 'We understand you are a scientist. You love your work. Do you really imagine a life of exile without conducting your experiments? We can give that to you.' He flashed his teeth. 'Sit. Rest your legs.'

He badly wanted to sit, to take the weight off his legs after the tour, which was basically a long painful walk on the road to boredom. But to sit with them? He would be lowering himself and expressing his acceptance of this farce. He could not do it. Better to stand tall and retain his honour. He fixed a sneer upon his face. 'Where's my niece? I want to see her.'

'On that, we have some bad news.'

She's dead. Skelos reached for the back of the chair to steady himself. *Brain dead probably from the journey through the rift.* 'Bad news?' *Now I truly am alone.*

'Yes,' said Halera. 'She has run away. Don't worry, we'll find her. She won't have gone far.'

He let out a relieved breath as he released the chair. He hoped for both their sakes she was running in his direction. He was disconcerted that she had managed a successful escape when he had failed to do the same. 'I've seen the state of this Kingdom. How could you have let her out of your sight? And you calmly sit here and talk to me about experiments.'

'You Citizens are quicker on your feet than us,' said a woman drenched in a royal blue robe and a gemstone clustered necklace.

'And she's small,' said a man with feathered eyebrows and loose skin around his jowls.

Both valid points. But she has my Shard. 'All the more reason to watch her more closely, I would have thought.'

'We're doing everything we can to find her,' said the large man, plunging his hand into a bowl of nuts and dried fruit. 'She won't have made it out of Baruch. We'll find her before the end of the day. I'm sure.' He tossed a handful of nuts into his mouth and once he had chewed and swallowed sufficiently, he spoke again. 'There are two important things you must know about this world. 'Firstly, there is no Citizen law here. Citizens live in secret. Anyone under the Shardner's service knows about Odisiris and the true nature of Citizens – the rest of the Narrigh population, to our knowledge, do not. The common folk of Narrigh will not understand or appreciate your kind. Therefore, you are forbidden from associating with non-Shardner members.'

Skelos feigned surprise by raising his brows, having already deduced his race were not as welcome as others. 'Do you intend to put me in chains and shackle me to a wall?'

His comment was ignored. The large man rested his elbows on the table and cupped his chin in both hands 'And secondly, it is a world without technology.'

A world without technology? What did that even mean? He couldn't imagine a society functioning without a necessity as essential as water. Odisiris had never known an era devoid of it. 'How am I to conduct experiments? Technology forms the fundamental basis for my experiments. It forms the fundamental basis of me.'

'I'm sure you can adapt.'

'I don't want to adapt,' he snapped. He shifted from one leg to another. 'I want off this planet immediately. There must be some mistake. I don't—'

A mistake or was this intentional? Osaphar had learned his secret and perhaps he was not alone. Without technology he was powerless.

Chapter 29

The two moons in the night sky caught Skelos's attention — a crescent moon to the east and a pearly white moon to the west. Two guards escorted him from the Royal Halls back into the bustling city streets.

The sounds of music and laughter filled the air, mixed with the clopping of horse hooves. The smells of the day were fading, replaced now by scents of alcohol, smoke, and sweat.

Skelos disliked it all. When a ragged boy approached with his hands out, Skelos slapped him hard, knocking the child to the ground. The boy scrambled away after a making some cursory comment.

Drunk men and women stumbled out of buildings with glass windows. Others sat chatting and laughing on flower-adorned balconies, or at tables laden with food and drink. He couldn't understand what they found so amusing in this chaotic place.

The guards led him through an arched gateway and down a sloping path to a door. Beyond were stairs and more doors, then stairs again. He lost count of how many. The guards ignored his questions about their destination.

He felt like he was in a dream, his legs the only parts still functioning. Sconces on the walls lit their way with flickering flames. The members of the Shardner council had not offered him a drink or food, nor did they give him their names. He could not get over how unimportant he was to them or their complacency over the fact Amelia was missing.

The slopes grew steeper. He nearly slipped on one slope when he spotted a hulking green figure. Man or alien, he couldn't say. It wore tattered pants and had a rusted chain and collar. Its face seemed crushed together. Its lips, eyes, and nose were squashed, teeth like fangs. The creature took no notice, and the guards showed no interest. Skelos struggled not to show his fear, not wanting to appear weak to the Unmarked Ones.

'What's the purpose of that thing?' he said in a hoarse whisper.

A young guard called Noec, with a domed forehead and wide-set eyes, gave Skelos a push which sent him careering down the slope. 'To make sure you don't try to escape.'

Skelos used his elbow to stop his fall against the door below. The two guards caught up and another unlocked the door, a glint of amusement in his eye.

Once through the door, the guards took Skelos down a set of steps and along a network of skewed rooms and corridors with black and copper walls. In one room they passed, he saw three guards poring over a crate set on a three-legged table fixed with metal studs. One held his painting aloft while his other hand sifted blindly through the crate in search of more treasures. Another was dismantling the microscope he had acquired from Dr Oliver Best.

He barged into the room and lunged at the guard holding his painting. 'That's mine!'

Suddenly, an invisible force threw him against the wall with a sharp pain in his chest. He landed on his side. The guard holding his painting glared at him while the other guard laughed.

Skelos struggled to his feet, coughing from having the wind knocked out of him. He was still trying to understand what just happened. Did the room have some kind of electromagnetic field or was there an issue with gravity? Or did he move so fast that he bounced off the wall himself? He had been walking for a while and was feeling unsteady on his feet.

'What are you doing?' he demanded, though he could feel himself blushing blue from embarrassment.

'Getting you to shut up, *Blue*,' said the guard who held the painting. He had now tucked it under his arm out of Skelos's reach. 'We weren't speaking to you.'

The guard wore battered boots and dented armour, though he had the bulk of a walrus. Still, Skelos knew the guard had not physically touched him. He knew better than to confront the guard further, as his body was not built for withstanding harm, whether by visible or invisible means.

'Where to?' asked Noec.

'Next left,' said the guard with the painting. 'Third door on the right.'

Noec tried to take Skelos by the arm. Skelos whipped his arm away.

As Skelos was leaving, he watched the guard in the dented breastplate hold the painting aloft. 'Callaway Castle for this one. It'll look nice against the drab background.'

'And what about this?' A guard held up the Shard Skelos had hidden in his robes before his arrival. 'This glass thing?'

'Put it in the vault,' replied the guard in the dented breastplate. 'The one that's always locked. Someone will get around to looking at it eventually.'

'Those are my possessions,' hissed Skelos.

'Not any more,' said Noec. 'They're the property of the Shardner now. I wouldn't make a fuss about it if I were you. You'll upset this lot. He nodded at the guards around the table. 'You don't want to do that. They might break something, like your legs.'

Skelos reigned in his anguish. 'What threw me against the wall back there? I was told technology was not permitted.'

'It's not,' said Noec. 'That was magic.'

'Magic is nothing more than an illusion,' he responded. 'It's not real.' Although the blow that was dealt him felt very real.

'It could be that magic is not real where you come from, but here it is as real as your *technology*.'

As they made their way along the passage, a putrid smell drifted up Skelos's nose. It was faint at first but grew stronger as they progressed. As did the noise: a mixture of squawking, flapping, and scratching.

He jerked his head back and pressed his hand to his mouth. The overpowering stench came from behind an iron door.

'Want to take a look?' said Noec.

He was at the door before Skelos could answer. He plunged a key through the keyhole and the door swung open.

The smell hit Skelos full on. It turned his stomach, making him heave.

Inside large crates were suspended from the ceiling by thick chains.

Noec laughed. 'The smell takes some getting used to.' He sauntered up to one crate. It slid across the floor, rose at one end, and then hit the ground again with a loud bang. 'You're a fiery one today. Aren't you, Marmaduke?' He turned to Skelos. 'I name them. Come take a look.'

'No.' Noec wanted to taunt and torture him. 'This place is disgusting. Take me to my laboratory. I don't see why we must loiter here.'

He glanced at the shaking crates above. *How secure are they?*

'You're afraid.'

'I most certainly am not,' he said, though his voice shook. 'Move out of my way.' He peered through a gap in the crate at a large bird with black wings and tusks. Its skin crawled with worms. 'What is it?'

'Dal-Carrion. Flesh eating beasts with a nasty bite. Now you'll have the chance to exercise your skills.'

'You want me to experiment on these?' He backed away in horror. The warehouse used to store the beasts went back further than his sharp eyes could see.

'No, on these.' Noec delved into his pocket and took out a winged-metal object. He handed it to Skelos.

'What do you expect me to do with this?'

'This is the device we use to capture them. A Herming Moth Wing. They're a breed of rare moth. It's where they get their name. Huge things. Thankfully, we don't see a lot of them in the Kingdom. The Dal-Carrion are dangerous and breeding fast. We want to conduct a test on at least twenty, maybe more.'

'What do the wings do exactly?'

'I just told you. They trap them.'

Skelos gazed at the Wing, then at the large crate beside Noec. He concluded that the subhuman was mad or drunk – possibly both. 'I'll need a demonstration.' If this was another one of their illusions, he would have to see it for himself.

'Stand back.' Noec tossed a handkerchief into the air along with the Wing.

Before Skelos could blink, the handkerchief vanished.

'Like magic,' Noec said with a smile. He opened the Wing to reveal the handkerchief caught within its folds, now torn down the middle. 'My best one, too.' He returned the ruined cloth to his pocket.

There is no such thing as magic. There is science or the Maker: the unexplained. 'Why do you want to study them?'

'I don't know why the Shardner want to study them, but I know they created them.'

'From what?'

'How should I know? You can keep that one.' He tossed Skelos the Herming Moth Wing.

Skelos let it drop to the ground. He had caught sight of Noec's grubby hands and did not want to touch him or the wing without his gloves. He pulled the sleeves of his robe down over his hands and awkwardly picked up the wing. He stowed it away. *I may find some use for it.*

'How many Dal-Carrions are out there?'

'Thousands.'

Chapter 30

He almost wept when he saw his new laboratory. There was nothing to it. It was smaller than his former wife's closet. It was furnished with a table, a joint basin, two stools, shelves stacked with archaic lab equipment, and a glass cabinet filled with small reptiles and furry brown creatures with short tails and long noses that he had never seen before.

A man in a wool coat stood in the laboratory. He had drooping eyelids, but shrewd eyes. He waited for Skelos to survey his new workspace for some time before introducing himself. 'I'm Tural, one of the supervisors here,' he said. He didn't smile, bow, or offer his hand.

Skelos couldn't care less for the phoney gestures of the unmarked. 'You expect me to work in here? Where is the energy source?' he said. 'There are no lights. What do you want me to do? Generate my own?'

'We have slow burners,' he gestured to the sconces on the wall. 'And oil lamps should you need them.'

'I can't work under these con-conditions alone.' And by alone he meant without the company of other Citizens.

'You'll have an assistant.'

'By assistant, I hope you mean a droid and not some simpering child.'

'As I said there is no technology here. You want technology – then invent it.'

'You want me to invent energy?'

'If you can manage to do it without the Shardner ever finding out, be my guest. In the meantime, use your theoretical knowledge to figure out how we can stop the Wings from springing open sporadically.'

These Unmarked are mad. Every last one of them.

'I was told I need to work on this.' He produced the Herming Moth Wing.

Tural nodded. 'Yes, they're not working as well as we had hoped. You see they were created by a sorcerer who used a special brand of magic. Unfortunately, he's dead. And the last doctor who tried to fix them has been disposed of. Faulty wings were not his area of expertise.'

Skelos was of the opinion that if one studied what was perceived as magic, a reasonable scientific explanation for its mysteries could always be found. He found no such explanation in the object presented to him: the Herming Moth Wing.

He selected a pair of surgical gloves from the table and slipped them on. He then banged the Herming Moth Wing on the table. Next, he held it up to his eye. It looked as if it was made from a blend of different metals: aluminium, copper, bronze, and countless more. He shook his head. *Preposterous.* 'I don't know what you expect me to do with this. I'm a scientist not a magician.'

'We don't think it's the magic that is at fault, but the metallic components used to create them. We thought you could adapt it somehow.'

Skelos stared at him dumbfounded. 'Adapt it from what? I don't know magic, and the equipment you have given me, if you can even call it that, is no good. You would need to harness the means of teleportation to trap the beasts. It's the only way you can replicate the

Wing's function. You said there was a doctor before me. What kind?'

'He specialised in genetic engineering.'

Then what did they expect? No doubt, I shall meet the same sorry end. 'This doctor of genetics you mentioned, his name doesn't happen to be Oliver Best, by any chance?'

Tural selected a microscope from one of the shelves and placed it on the table. 'Yes. I didn't know the two of you had met.'

Skelos cleared his throat. He would not have believed Oliver's account of how he arrived in the Red Caves if he had told him then or now. 'What you're asking is nothing short of manual labour. I'm a neuroscientist, not an engineer or an ironmonger. I don't know anything about metals and magic.'

This wasn't true. He had studied metals as part of his neurorobotics research, but such metals appeared not to exist in Narrigh.

'You use metals for your neurorobotics.'

'I never made cyborgs, you fool. I only enhanced their capabilities.'

'Is the premise not the same? You have the Wings. All you need to do is modify them. You can use the specimens in the cabinet as case studies. We can obtain other materials for you, should you need them. Your apprentice will be here shortly. The Wings are the Shardner's greatest priority.'

'More of a priority than my niece, I suppose.'

'Forgive me,' said Tural. He gave a small bow. 'Of course, finding your niece is our highest priority.'

Skelos rolled his eyes as he slotted the Wing under the microscope. It would be quite an achievement for him, as a neuroscientist, to fix magical metallic wings. Yet part of him felt compelled to try, if only to prove his intellectual capabilities ran deeper than even he realised. Success would show his resilience in adapting to this strange new world he now found himself in. Yes, it truly was the Maker's Will that he should come here.

He sighed, still harbouring a hope of escaping. Surely at some point an airship would arrive, one he could stow away on. And Amelia—she possessed a cunning spirit when motivated. With her help, he may find a way off this world. Then there was the matter of the Avu'lore artifact and its mysterious powers. If he could only locate the scattered Shards and reassemble them, then he could put the artefact to use.

He clung to the notion that the day would come. And when it did, he would applaud it.

Science Fantasy series, THE OTHER WORLDS

Skelos Dorm's adventures continue in *The Quest of Narrigh, The Plague of Pyridian* and *The Chancellor of Odisiris*

To learn more about **The Other Worlds** visit tridanentertainment.com

Excerpt from *The Quest of Narrigh*

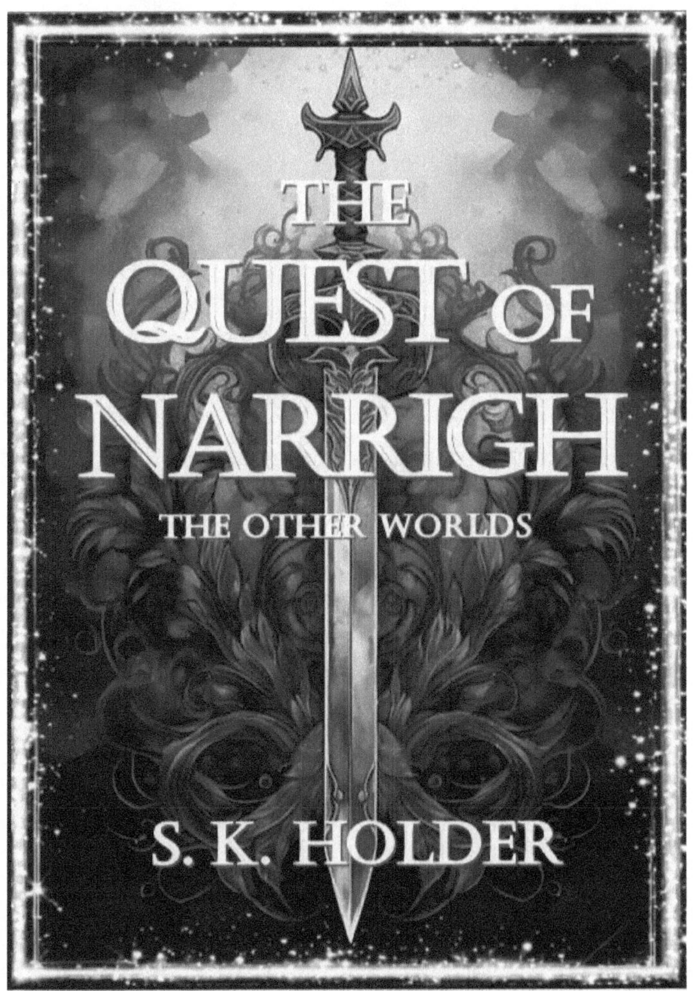
THE
QUEST OF
NARRIGH
THE OTHER WORLDS
S. K. HOLDER

Chapter 1

It had happened on a Saturday.

Connor hadn't had much sleep the night before. He was all jittery with excitement. He had risen early to hang out the washing his mum had left in a basket on the kitchen table. He even completed his brother's chores: sweeping the kitchen floor and putting out the rubbish. After he was done, he sat in the living room, idly flicking through one of his old comic books. His best friend Riley was coming over.

Connor's mum was at work, which meant he could do whatever he wanted in the house as long as he didn't invade his brother's personal space. Connor planned to do that later when his brother had left for the cinema with his friends and before his mum returned. 'The Quest' would be his and Riley's to play.

The Quest of Narrigh was the biggest massively multi-player online role-playing game ever to be released by Tridan Entertainment. Its creators had deposited so many obstacles, that any player would be lucky to reach Level Twenty.

His fifteen-year-old brother, Luke, sauntered into the room. He was on the phone with his friend, Walter 'Bat' Bateman. 'Yeah Bat. Level Forty....told you I'd do it.'

Connor flung down his comic book, his eyes wide, his mouth gaping open. He had a name for the way he constantly regarded his brother; he called it the Look of Awe. Luke seemed to appreciate Connor staring at him as if he were some sort of comic book hero. 'Wow! You got to Level Forty.'

Luke nodded, a smug grin on his face. 'Yeah, yeah I know,' he spoke into the phone. 'But it was me who put in the extra work. My fingers need a break though...laptop's playing up. I think it's overheated. What time will you get here?'

His brother had reached Level Forty in thirty-eight hours. Not bad.

Luke had allowed him enough game play to get some idea of the skill involved. Connor reckoned he could reach Level Forty in a lot less time than that, if he had more free time on his hands, if he could stay up late, if he had a computer in his bedroom. He had to share a laptop with his mum. It didn't help that she made full use of the parental controls, which prevented him from freely surfing the internet.

Luke ended the call and shoved the phone into his back pocket. 'You like that, huh? One day, I'll show you how it's done. What time's Riley coming over?'

'Twelve.'

Luke gave him a weary grin and then leaned over and ruffled his hair. His brother was such a sap. 'You stay here or in your room, understand?'

'I know. Why do you always have to tell me?'

Luke shrugged. 'Because.'

Because five years ago, Connor had packed a bag and gone in search of the dad he had never met, and whose name he couldn't remember. He knew he was never going to find him, but he didn't care. His mum had told him off for using her bottle of shampoo in his water-gun, and his brother had been ignoring him all day. He had left the house in a huff, having packed a change of clothes and some of his favourite toys and books. He was going to take the bus into town, but he didn't have any money. It was late and he had soon grown tired. His bag was heavy because of all the books he was carrying, and people were staring at him. When a woman in a trenchcoat asked him if he was okay, he ran into the park to get away from her. And that's where his brother found him, curled up on the grass, cradling his toy truck.

Luke had given him a clout round the ear for causing him and his mum to worry. Connor promised them that he would never run away again. He intended to honour that promise. Deep down, he didn't mind his mum and brother treating him like a baby. He wasn't ready to grow up.

He gave Luke the Look of Awe. 'Can Riley and I watch you game today?'

'Don't see why not.'

Connor grinned and reached for his comic book. Yes, the Look of Awe definitely came in handy.

As soon as Luke and his friends had tumbled out of the door, Connor didn't hesitate. He switched off the TV and skulked upstairs to his brother's bedroom with Riley following close behind.

Connor sunk into the swivel chair and wheeled himself up to the desk. He turned on the laptop.

Riley pulled up a chair next to him. 'Won't your mum say something if she catches us in here?'

Connor pulled a tattered sheet of paper from his pocket. 'Yep.'

'What's that?' Riley rested his chin on Connor's shoulder. His chestnut locks tickled the side of Connor's face.

'Luke's password combos. He only uses five, so it should be easy.' Connor had watched his brother while away the hours at his computer enough times to memorise all five passwords, one of which was Connor's own name.

Riley took the sheet of paper from him. He turned it over. 'And what's this on the back?'

'Notes to get us started.' They weren't much. He had picked up a few smart moves from watching his brother play.

'They don't make any sense.'

Connor whipped the paper from his hand. 'They make sense to me.'

Riley placed two cans of soft drink on the desk. 'What's wrong with the screen?'

The screen was flashing a luminous purple. Connor dusted it off with the palm of his hand and then tapped the ESCAPE key. The screen returned to normal. 'Seen too much action, I guess. And it's about to see some more.'

Connor logged into the game and pressed PLAY.

The Lands of Narrigh

"Eight hundred years ago, in the Age of Peace, Narrigh, once collectively known as the Goldlands had eight regions: Narrul, Hizsen, Garnorm, Theris, Baruch, Crinol, Shile and Olvastan.

To the North, lay Garnorm and Hizsen. Garnorm was inhabited by a race of humans known as the Gamnod, who were gifted in the crafts of counselling, sculpting, and tailoring.

The Darque Goblins dwelled in Hizsen and were renowned for their camouflage and enchanting skills.

The Isles of Crinol were surrounded by the blue waters of the Hizsen Sea. Here the Drone Elves dwelled. They were exceptional potion-makers and flame-wielders.

In the Etbur mountains of Crinol, dwelled the Traceless who had no name and no soul to speak of.

To the west, lay Narrul, home to the dwarves, who were famed for their mining and iron-forging skills.

To the South, lay Olvastan, where there dwelled humans, who believed in one God as opposed to the Gamnod who believed in many. The people of Olvastan were great farmers and tradesmen.

Further South, in the Shile region, there lived the gypsy clans, known for their herbal remedies and hunting skills.

To the East, lay the Kingdom of Baruch, bathed in gold and home to King Kalgar and Queen Irentha. The King and Queen ruled Narrigh with an iron-hand to maintain its prosperity and tranquillity. Their Score Army was both revered and feared.

Not far from the Kingdom of Baruch was Theris, home to the Theria Elves, who worked tirelessly to weave beautiful cloth and textiles for all Narrigh. They were also renowned for their enchantments.

One day, evil descended on the lands of Narrigh. It came in the form of a heatwave. It started with a flush of red in the sky, which rapidly simmered to a burnt orange and then a sun-soaked yellow. It descended on the land like some great floodlight, burning fire-bright and smothering the lands with a haze of shimmering heat.

A heat that was unbearable. It sent races and beasts alike scuttling to their homes, seeking shade where they could find it.

Some months later, a strong breeze swept across Narrigh. It cooled the land with its charm-less icy breath. Rain followed, marking an end to the drought, bringing the inhabitants of Narrigh out into the open.

A great rainbow formed in the sky. The people of Olvastan marvelled at its beauty, saying it was a gift from God to announce the beginnings of a bountiful harvest to come. The Theria Elves believed it was a gift from the Elfin Spirit, King Garlor, for their crafts. The Gamnod race thought the rainbow had been created by the Old One, whom they called Uom, to show them the way to a new world. The dwarves believed the rainbow was wondrous and that if they bathed in its arc, they would find mountains of gold and other riches. The Darque Goblins, however, feared the rainbow was an omen, marking the end of peace in their time.

And the Darque Goblins were right.

The rainbow stood in the sky for four days. On the fifth day, it faded as a smile fades on the lips, spitting fire and rock. It carved a great crater in the North. It poisoned the Garn Ocean and the Hizsen Sea. Many died. All lost their homes.

The surviving Gamnod people and the Darque Goblins appealed to the King and Queen of Baruch to give them aid, to let them seek sanctuary within the Kingdom.

King Kalgar and Queen Irentha believed that because the Poison Rainbow had wreaked so much damage over Garnorm and Hizsen, the Gamnod people, and the Darque Goblins must have done something terrible to anger their Gods. They also deemed that their customs and religions had no place in the other regions of Narrigh. Hence, the King and Queen granted them little aid and refused them entry to the southern, eastern, and western regions. They also had their Score Army erect a barrier named, Shile Point to prevent their passage. A gate to the North, it sat on the edge of the Dead Forest.

The Darque Goblins and the Gamnod were hurt and angry that the King and Queen had abandoned them. Evil rose in their minds and consumed them. They sought an alliance with the Traceless and the Drone Elves to help them gain vengeance over the Baruchians.

And so, the Age of War came.

From this war sprung two factions: the Furnace and the Storm.

The Furnace faction of the North formed the Blade Army. The Blade Army invaded the Kingdom of Baruch, and thus a great battle ensued between the Furnace faction and the Score Army. The Score Army were outnumbered. The kingdom was defeated, and the King and the Queen put to death. The Furnace held the Kingdom for three years until the Storm faction formed of Garnorm humans, Theria Elves and dwarves, drove the Furnace's Blade Army back North and restored the Kingdom back to the Baruchians.

Hizsen became known as the Great Northern Crater and the races of the North became fewer and scattered.

After the Age of Wars comes the Age of Trepidation.

The Shardner government seeks to protect the races of four regions: Theris, Olvastan, Baruch, and Narrul, who remain forever wary of the North. They believe its lands are cursed. The threat of another northern invasion hangs over them. The fear of another Poison Rainbow weighs heavy on their minds."

"Far beyond the Poison Rainbow, lies the world of Odisiris, predominately occupied by a race known as Citizen. It is from here that the Poison Rainbow evolved. Unbeknown to the races of Narrigh, the rainbow created a rift between their world and the world of Odisiris.

The creator of these worlds knows of the rift and seeks to use it to his advantage. He hopes others do not seek to do the same. For he holds in his possession, a great artefact that if wielded, could disrupt the balance of the two worlds and ultimately lead to their destruction."

Connor hastily scrolled through the game's background story. 'I can't believe they try to hold up your game play with this crap.' He took a slurp of drink from the can. 'We don't need to know all this stuff.'

He set to work creating his own player character: a human warrior with his own suit of leather armour and a Lightning Sword to help blast his enemies to smithereens. He knew warriors fought a lot and were brave. There was no time to read up on any other Professions. He would have to pick the rest up as he went along. He had not forgotten that his mum, who had returned home from work, was taking a nap and could wake up at any moment.

'Can't we just play your brother's character, Duffy?' Riley frowned at the screen. 'It'll save time.'

'Rookie mistake. If we don't want him to suspect anything, we need to create a new character, one we can delete when we're done.' Not that his brother would ever suspect him of foul play.

Riley guzzled from his can of soda. 'What good is that? We'll have to start all over again, every time he goes out. Just play Luke's character.'

Connor scowled at him. Riley was taking away all the excitement with his moaning. 'No. You don't mess with another player's character. You don't do that. Don't you know anything about the sacred code of gaming?'

Riley bowed his head. 'Only what you teach me, O Great One.'

Connor smirked. He didn't know anything about the sacred code of gaming either. He knew he didn't want to snatch Luke's personal victory away from him; he just wanted to beat it. And in time, he would. His brother need never know. 'Okay. I'll create a new character and I won't delete it. If he sees it, he'll think Bat put it there.'

Riley gave a nod and two short burps. 'Then I want my own character too.'

Chapter 2

Someone was talking to him, prising him out of the shell he called sleep. The voice was gruesomely loud. Pivotal.

'Northern beasts. Get up!'

Connor woke to find himself in the hollow stump of a tree. He was dressed in strange clothes: a leather tunic over a linen shirt, wool trousers, and soggy brown boots. There was a leather bag strapped across his shoulder and a thin metal chain around his neck. The beating of a thousand wings pounded in his ears.

'Riley?'

The stump moved. Someone or something was shaking it.

He tried to reassure himself. 'I'm still dreaming. I haven't really woken up.' That happened in dreams sometimes. You wake from one dream only to find yourself in another.

He attempted to steady the stump with his hands. The stump was slippery with moss and yellow fungus. He jerked his head from side to side, willing himself to wake. He gave his hand a hard, quick pinch. When his skin snapped back into place, a patch appeared that looked almost black beneath his brown skin. Regardless, the pinch had no impact on his current dilemma.

A grimy tusk flashed in front of his eyes. His dreams had never felt this real, or his nightmares. There was something out there.

Blood rushed through his veins, thawing out his stiff limbs, sharpening his senses. Northern beasts?

The last he remembered, he had been playing *The Quest of Narrigh* on his brother's computer with his friend, Riley.

He must have dropped off to sleep.

He gave a loud gasp as a white-hot pain exploded in his ankle. A beast with a beak honed like a steel sword had taken hold of his right foot, clamping down on his flesh, crushing it. The size of the beast's head was three times the size of his own. On either side of its beak were two great tusks.

He breathed through clenched teeth, fighting to push back the pain. He had to dislodge himself from the tree trunk fast.

The beast casually lowered its head and peered in. Its yellow eyes fastened on its victim. Very slowly, it began to reel in its prey.

He fought to gather his wits. He braced himself against the trunk and desperately tried to draw himself up to the other end of the stump. The creature responded by forcibly pinching his ankle, determined to drag its squirming-meal out from its 'wooden container'.

His foot twisted and then cracked. He arched his back. His strangled cry echoed through the tree hollow. 'Come on,' he spat. 'Come on!' His eyes watered. Bracing himself again, he lashed out with his free leg. The beast moved to skewer it with its tusk.

He swung his leg away, snagging his trousers. He clawed at the bark, fighting the pain, vehemently trying to blot it out. He gave a deep-throated growl and, with one vicious kick, struck the beast's beak with his foot.

It opened its jaws, releasing his leg, which smacked the ground with a grisly thud.

He exerted all his energy into scrambling from the trunk. He wrenched himself up, only to find two of the great, seething beasts closing in on either side of him. Maggots dripped from the folds of their wings.

He staggered away, grimacing in pain. He was afraid his injured ankle would give out on him; afraid he wouldn't make it. Instead, he found his strides lengthening.

Very soon, he was running through a forest locked in shadow, his sodden boots squelching in the soil, the wind whistling past his ears.

Squawking noisily, the beasts rose into the air.

He spotted a boy just ahead of him, running low to the ground with his bloodied hands wrapped around his head. One of the beasts was on his tail, lunging at him with its talons.

He cast about the forest floor, looking for something to ward it off. He grabbed a sturdy, forked tree branch and charged at the wings of the swooping beast. If he could divert its attention, the boy could get away.

Wallop!

He found himself face down in the soil, floored by a blow from the beast's wing. He scrambled for his piece of tree branch to find it had fallen well out of reach.

Three of the rancid smelling beasts ensnared him. They cocked their heads and sunk their shiny pink claws into the forest floor.

A chill went through his spine. *They're going to eat me.* One night, he had hidden behind the sofa when his brother and his friends were watching a horror film about a man-eating bird. He had nightmares about it for months afterwards.

One of the beasts struck him on the side of the head with its beak. His punishment, he supposed, for trying to outrun them. He clenched his jaw. The pain penetrated his skull. Black and silver sparks flashed before his eyes.

The beasts set to work, scraping away soil from around him with their wiry claws, showering him with maggots. He felt himself sinking on a wet platform. Soil rained down on him in thick wet clumps, blocking his airways.

He would need to act quickly before they buried him alive.

Wheezing and coughing, he heaved himself onto his side and pulled the straps of his bag from around his shoulders.

Then without looking, without thinking, he tore the bag open and drew from it the first thing he could lay his hands on - an apple, soft and bruised. He flung the piece of fruit at the beasts. It missed them. He watched in horror as the lime green apple disappeared into the ground.

The beasts commenced using their beaks to break up the soil even faster.

Tears stung Connor's eyes. 'I can feel the cold shadow of death upon my face.' That was what the man had said in the film when the giant bird had started gnawing on his neck.

If this was a dream, wasn't it about time he woke up?

'You ran away again. Don't you remember?' said an Authoritative Voice inside his head. 'You wanted to come here.'

He fought to regain his reasoning. *What if I am in Narrigh?*

A Warrior had been his chosen Profession. He didn't have his armour, his Lightning Sword, or the enchanted shield he won in Level Fifteen. He raised his hands and thrust out his fingers. No light shot from them. No orbs of flame.

The thing around his neck! With determined fury, he grappled with his shirt collar. His fingers slid along the thin metal chain. Suspended from it was an egg-shaped pendant. There were bands set in the Egg's middle encrusted with gemstones. Instinctively, he took the band between his finger and thumb and rotated it in a frenzy. 'Help me, please!'

Just when he started to believe his instincts had failed him, a spectacular bolt of blue light shot from the pendant, pierced the air, and then vanished.

Screeching in fright, the beasts took to the sky, soaring above the treetops and out of sight.

Coughing up the last of the soil from his throat, he reached for his bag and hauled himself from the pit. He hobbled away without looking back.

The reality of the world around him grew starker and more perilous in his mind.

Chapter 3

Meanwhile, elsewhere on Narrigh...

The world of Narrigh is alien to Citizens. Technology is ubiquitous where they come from. They rely on it for their very existence. How well they can cope without it, in these extraordinary lands, only time will tell.

Skelos's moment of glory had almost slipped through his fingers like the intangible dreams of the wretched victims on which he conducted his experiments.

Almost.

He was in the Shardner's custody, exiled from Odisiris to a foreign land. They had put him to work on the Herming Moth Wings. Supposedly, his predecessor's invention was faulty. What did they expect when he had specimens no bigger than lizards on which to test them?

The Shardner will keep me here forever, out of sight, but unfortunately not out of mind.

He wiped the sweat and grime from his face and threw another metal Wing into the crate, sneaking a glance at the door where two guards were stationed. Half-crazed with weariness, they were still upright. Their shift would end in twenty minutes. He would get five minutes respite before a new set of guards came on duty, and he could get little done in five minutes, very little in this pitiful excuse for a lab. The laboratory was not designed with comfort in mind, nor was it designed to allow a scientist or his designated assistant to indulge in their scientific passions. The furniture was conventional, the utensils basic. There was a standard lab table, a double bowl sink, two stools and shelves stacked with beakers, test tubes, flasks, spoons, tongs and one microscope. In the corner stood a tall glass cabinet, which housed three groups of specimens: orange lizards, snout-nosed Ticket Shrews, and miniature red frogs.

Bored and agitated, Skelos lined-up the beakers on the nearest and lowest shelf to him. He had sent his assistant home an hour ago.

He had chosen to wear his favourite purple silk-lined robes rather than don the clinical black coat more suited to his Profession. The robes hid his widening girth, which was about all they were good for. He had tripped over and snagged the fabric more times than he could count.

Truth be told, he had no idea how to fix the Wings, and furthermore, he did not care. He was done with all this. He was superior to the races of Narrigh, a Citizen. First Status. Why should he work for them?

He strutted up to one of the guards and tapped him on the shoulder. The guard swatted away Skelos's fat finger with the steel baton he clutched in his hand, his face a rigid mask. He was a burly fellow with cauliflower ears and a crooked mammoth-sized nose. His ill-fitted black tunic bulged at the seams. Another Unmarked One[1], mused Skelos, who didn't see fit to bow.

'What?' said the guard.

'I wondered if you could fetch me something from the Stores.'

'Ain't no fetcher,' said the guard.

Skelos gazed at his companion who shrugged. 'You've been given everything you need, so get on with it.'

The other guard was a Second Status Citizen, with all the arrogance of a First. He had dark brown skin, an athletic build, sinewy muscles and an angular jaw. *Now, he could prove to be a problem.*

'And how would you know what I need?' Skelos asked, inwardly seething.

The guards kept quiet. Skelos knew what was going through their minds. The store was ten minutes away at a jog; a Citizen might make it there in three minutes. However, once there, they would have to wait for him to find what he needed in the extensive storerooms, get security clearance and sign the logbook. All of which took time. Their shift would overrun, and they were not getting paid overtime to babysit.

'My assistant forgot to bring me a valuable ingredient,' said Skelos, 'and these Wings won't wait.'

The guards looked at each other. The Herming Moth Wings were a priority, every serving member of the Shardner knew it.

'We're not to leave our posts,' said the Burly One.

'Perhaps one of you can escort me to the Stores.' Skelos stared hopefully into the Burly One's eyes. *Please let it be you.*

'You go, Vastra,' said the Burly One to his fellow guard. 'Make it quick. I want to be out of here on time.'

The other guard cocked his head at Skelos and pulled open the metal door. 'Let's go.'

The guard, named Vastra, hurried Skelos down the passage. 'What's the matter with you? Can't you go any faster?' he barked, waiting for Skelos to catch him up.

'No, I'm afraid I can't.' Skelos hunched a little and coughed, an act, which seemed to infuriate Vastra further.

'It's a good thing you've got brains or the Shardner would have been rid of you long ago. Now hurry the blazes up!'

Skelos refused to be rushed. The Avu'lore he had hidden in his robes was slowing him down, making him hobble, making him wish he had lifted a few more weights and eaten a lot less pies. He could not leave it behind. It was his most prized possession, his only possession of any worth.

As Vastra said, he had brains.